GIRL MISSING

A DETECTIVE KAITLYN CARR MYSTERY

KATE GABLE

BYRD BOOKS LLC

COPYRIGHT

Proofreaders:

Julie Deaton, Deaton Author Services, https://www.facebook.com/jdproofs/

Renee Waring, Guardian Proofreading Services, https://www.facebook.com/GuardianProofreadingServices

Savanah Cotton, Cotton's Incision Editing, https://www.facebook.com/Cottons-Incision-Editing-512917856115256/

Cover Design: Kate Gable

Visit my website at www.kategable.com

WANT TO BE THE FIRST TO KNOW ABOUT MY UPCOMING SALES, NEW RELEASES AND EXCLUSIVE GIVEAWAYS?

Sign up for my newsletter: https://www.subscribepage.com/kategableviplist

Join my Facebook Group: https://www.facebook.com/groups/833851020557518

Bonus Points: Follow me on BookBub and Goodreads!

https://www.goodreads.com/author/show/21534224.Kate_Gable

ABOUT KATE GABLE

Kate Gable loves a good mystery that is full of suspense. She grew up devouring psychological thrillers and crime novels as well as movies, tv shows and true crime.

Her favorite stories are the ones that are centered on families with lots of secrets and lies as well as many twists and turns. Her novels have elements of psychological suspense, thriller, mystery and romance.

Kate Gable lives in Southern California with her husband, son, a dog and a cat. She has spent more than twenty years in this area and finds inspiration from its cities, canyons, deserts, and small mountain towns.

Write her here:

Kate@kategable.com

Check out her books here:

www.kategable.com

Sign up for my newsletter:

https://www.subscribepage.com/kategableviplist

Join my Facebook Group:
https://www.facebook.com/
groups/833851020557518

Bonus Points: Follow me on BookBub and Goodreads!

https://www.bookbub.com/authors/kate-gable

https://www.goodreads.com/author/show/
21534224.Kate_Gable

amazon.com/Kate-Gable/e/B095XFCLL7
facebook.com/kategablebooks
bookbub.com/authors/kate-gable
instagram.com/kategablebooks

ALSO BY KATE GABLE

All books are available at ALL major retailers! If you can't find it, please email me at **kate@kategable.com**

Girl Missing (Book 1)

Girl Lost (Book 2)

Girl Found (Book 3)

Girl Taken (Book 4)

Girl Forgotten (Book 5)

Girl Hidden (FREE Novella)

ABOUT GIRL MISSING

Don't lie to me...

A young girl from a wealthy family is found hanging from a tree in a secluded canyon.

What was she doing there in the middle of the night? How did she get there? Who did this to her? **Detective Kaitlyn Carr is determined to find out and bring the killer to justice.**

But when her thirteen-year-old sister vanishes on her way back from a friend's house, Kaitlyn must split her time and confront demons from her own past in order to bring her sister home.

The small mountain town of Big Bear Lake is only three hours away but a world away from her life in Los Angeles. It's the place she grew up and the place that's plagued her with lies, death and secrets.

As Kaitlyn digs deeper into both cases, she finds out that appearances are misleading and few things are what they seem.

A murderer is lurking in the shadows and the more of the mystery that Kaitlyn unspools the closer she gets to danger herself.

Can Kaitlyn find the killer and solve the mystery of her sister's disappearance before it's too late?

What happens when someone else is taken?

Girl Missing is a suspenseful thriller filled for fans of A. J. Rivers, Mary Stone, Willow Rose, James Patterson, Melinda Leigh, Kendra Elliot, Ella Gray, and Karin Slaughter. It has mystery, angst, a bit of romance and family drama.

1

I should not be here. I make my way down the uneven terrain, careful not to twist my ankle. Officers are already gathered at the front, securing the crime scene. Tape has been put up. Out in the distance, the full moon hovers over me, an ominous sign of what I'm about to uncover.

Dispatch provided me with the basic facts, but it's my job to put together the story, not just the story, the truth.

A dog walker found a young girl hanging from a tree and cut her down in hopes of resuscitating her.

I approach the scene swiftly, but carefully. The morning run that I took hours ago is now catching up with me. I've been meaning to get into better shape for the last few years, starting and stopping various exercise regimes.

This week I have made a commitment. This is my third day in a row, the longest that I have stuck with it. As a result, my calves are tight and it feels like I'm lifting cement blocks with each step.

The girl's body is located up a steep hill, just around an enormous granite boulder. I step over rocks, slipping slightly on the gravel. I am careful to avoid touching the bulging roots of the pine tree as I struggle to the crime scene.

I introduce myself and flash my badge. The officer who was the first to arrive on the scene gives me a slight nod and shows me the body.

The pine trees in these parts don't have too many low hanging branches and this one is almost ten feet off the ground. The rope is tied tightly to it and I see the spot where the dog walker cut her down.

The thick white rope is frayed at the ends. I follow the trajectory of how she would have fallen and I see her lying flat on her back, eyes open staring up.

Her hair is matted, but at one point it had been a beautiful flaxen blonde. Her eyes have winged eyeliner and perfectly applied eyelashes. The lipstick around her mouth is smeared, but it doesn't look like she had been crying.

The crime scene technicians are already gathering evidence and I stand a little bit back examining everything from a distance.

“So, you are the one who found her?" I ask, turning to Keith Upton, a doughy man with pink cheeks and a receding hairline.

He's desperately trying to hold onto his beagle, who is barking nonstop at every single person walking by. I take a few steps closer to them, kneel down, and give the dog my hands to sniff.

“Wow, my dog doesn't like anyone,” Keith says.

"Tell me how you found her,” I ask, pulling out a small notebook and a pen.

“Well,” he hesitates, “I was walking right here like we always do. Lucky needs a lot of exercise so that he doesn't destroy everything in the house. He's only a puppy, you know.”

“Uh-huh.” I nod.

“I usually like to go on a hike right behind my house on the Willow Creek trail.”

“Yes.” I nod. “What was different about today?”

"I don't know. I was talking on the phone with my brother-in-law and we got into a really heated political discussion. I needed to blow off some steam. I just don't get it, you know. How can any people vote for people like that?"

"So, that's why you ended up coming here?" I ask, trying to steer him back on track.

"Yes, there's a trail right over there. I know that dogs aren't allowed off the leash here, but there was no one around and she needed the exercise. So, I threw the ball a couple of times up the hill away from the trail and then it got lost. She came back without it. I told her to go look. I didn't really want to leave the trail, but she couldn't find it and it was the last one I had."

"And?" I ask.

I'm tempted to fill in the blank and just say, "So, that's how you found her?" but I don't want to put words in his mouth.

All of these details seem mundane, but cases are solved in the weeds. I need to know everything that Keith can remember because I don't know what the clue will be that helps me find out the truth.

"I left the trail and let Lucky lead me over to where I thought I'd thrown the ball. That's when I saw *her*." He gasps and gets choked up. "Just hanging there. Swaying in the wind. Her body was so small, she practically looked like a scarecrow. God, I shouldn't have said that. That's awful."

"No, details like that are important. I want to be able to see what you saw."

Then suddenly, the strong, confident façade of this nonchalant man breaks down. He turns away from me to hide the tears streaming from his eyes.

"It's okay," I say calmly, touching him lightly on the arm. "It's going to be okay."

"I've never seen a dead body before," he says, and this actually catches me by surprise. He must be at least in his fifties. Hasn't he ever been to a funeral?

"I've never even been to a funeral. I guess I'm lucky that way. I've never had much family, but my parents are still around, healthy, and I don't know anyone who has died since my grandparents did when I was a baby."

I continue to pat his forearm, trying to figure out a way to steer this conversation back on course. So far, I have found out way too much information about the man who found the dead girl, but not so much about the dead girl herself.

"I cut her down," Keith suddenly says, his voice cracking. "I thought that maybe she was still breathing, like maybe I could save her, but I should have looked closer. I should've seen how cold she was."

He shakes his head and starts to rock his body from side to side. It's a common thing for people who want to soothe themselves.

"Why did you have a knife?" I ask.

"I always carry one with me in my bag. When we go on long walks like this, one or two hours, my blood sugar drops and I will bring an apple or an orange as a backup, but I don't like biting into apples. I prefer to cut them into slices."

He opens his bag and pulls one out.

"We will have to take it as evidence," I say.

"The apple?" He gasps.

I almost laugh.

"No, the knife and the bag."

"Oh, yes, of course. When will I get it back?"

"I'm not exactly sure. It will really depend on how this case proceeds, but I wouldn't expect it back anytime soon."

I don't ask him any more questions, for now. Instead, I walk around the scene, taking it all in. It's not very late in the afternoon, but the sun is already setting. The mountains around here are tall, casting long shadows over the valley. It's winter, after all.

"Detective Carr." An eager young deputy approaches me. He has to be in his early twenties at the most, but he looks like a kid of fifteen dressed like a cop for Halloween.

"There's something else here," he says as I read the shiny, polished name tag on his chest.

Officer Gary Lenore's uniform is freshly pressed and his shoes continue to shine as if they have just been polished, despite all of the dust on the trail. We all know how uncomfortable those dress shoes can be and I'm pleased that I haven't heard him complain about it once, not even to his friend.

Lenore leads me over around the tree where an extensive root structure is peeking out of the ground. The towering pine with its reddish trunk looks like it's about to tip over at any moment, but it continues to stand and probably will still be here long after we're all gone.

Lenore points to something on the ground and I lean in for a closer look. It's a couple of twenties folded in half that look like they have just fallen out of someone's pocket.

The photographer comes over to document what we have found and the crime technician places them into an evidence bag. I take my own picture with my phone, for personal record keeping.

I walk back around to the girl. No one has moved her. Luckily, no one draped anything over her body and contaminated the scene either.

You'd think that given what we all know from watching endless CSI shows no one would make a mistake like that anymore, let alone people who work in police departments, but we had someone do just that exact same thing to a victim out in Victorville last year.

The covering of the body tends to happen more often in cases when the victim is female and nude.

In this case, the girl is dressed in plaid pajama pants and an oversized t-shirt, something you'd wear at home or perhaps to go to bed. The evenings have gotten quite cool with temperatures dipping down into the low 50s, but there is no jacket.

Another thing that stands out are her flip-flops. Bright pink, plastic, resembling a thong, separating her big toe from the rest of the foot. Her toenails are painted turquoise, a very neat job, not the way that I used to paint my nails when I was a kid. There's a good possibility that they were done professionally, whether or not this has anything to do with the case, I have no idea.

"You see the flip-flops." I turn to Lenore.

He nods, eager to learn.

"Well, it has been in the 70s during the day, but it's too cold for them now, right? Besides, who would choose that to wear on a hike to commit suicide?"

He nods, but he doesn't seem convinced.

"You don't agree?" I ask.

"No, you're probably right. What do I know?" He shrugs.

"Tell me," I say. "Tell me what you're thinking."

I have never been one of those cops whose opinion couldn't be challenged. In fact, I welcome it. I'm not a pushover, but I also know that I don't know everything.

I've also known many bad detectives who come onto a scene and make a snap judgement right away and go out of their way to collect evidence that proves them right. I don't plan on going down that rabbit hole.

No, you have to approach every scene with an open mind and an open heart. Anything could have happened. The victim can't tell you the truth, but the evidence can and I'm not just talking about DNA. There are other details: how the victim's clothing is arranged, the position of the body, and in this case, how the rope is tied.

"So, the thing about the flip-flops is that she could have worn them because some girls tend to do that," Lenore says. "My little sister is obsessed. She wears them all the time. It hardly matters what the weather is so, unless it drops down into the thirties, she always has them on."

"How old is your sister?" I ask.

"Twelve."

I glance over at the girl. She can't be older than fourteen. It's hard to tell though. When you're dead, you look older than you are in real life.

I make my way around the tree again. A few people gather by the plastic partition around the crime scene. There are hikers who have come upon the investigation and there are others who have heard the commotion from below the trail and come up. Occasionally, we ask these people to leave, but it's not uncommon for the person who had something to do with the death to stick around.

I approach three deputies standing in a huddle, gossiping.

"It has to be a suicide," the bigger one, who had interviewed the dog walker earlier, insists. "Otherwise, she'd be naked and sexually assaulted, but it doesn't look like her clothes were even removed."

"Where is the ladder?" I ask.

"Excuse me?" He turns to face me.

His short, cropped hair is completely flat on top giving his head a strange rectangular look. His face is freckled and his demeanor is cocky, well above his rank. Pay grade and arrogance typically have a positive correlation, but this guy is an outlier even for that range.

"There must be a ladder, right? Especially if we suspect that this was a suicide."

I use the word *we* intentionally, pausing to enunciate it. It's one of the tricks of the trade. If I say *you*, it's an accusation, which can possibly be taken personally. If I say *we*, then I'm referring to no one in particular and everyone is at fault.

"There is no ladder," the skinny deputy says, nervously shifting his weight from one foot to another.

"That would make it difficult to have been a suicide then," I say quietly.

I am sure of this fact, but I have to play these little games of semantics in order to keep everyone's egos in check.

"The rope was tied up on that branch." I point. "I'm not exactly sure how far off the ground it is, but this girl could not climb up there without a ladder or help."

"So, this is a murder?" Lenore asks.

"Looks like it." I nod.

I jot down a few notes in my notebook and take a few more pictures with my phone. The photos help me remember things, small details, something that I might overlook.

I scan the scene again.

Is there anything in her pockets? Did she have a phone?

I won't know the answers to any of these questions until the scene is properly processed and that's not my job.

Despite all the advances in technology, my job remains pretty straightforward. I ask people questions and I make sure the answers make sense. When they don't, I ask more questions.

Taking a few steps away from the body, I point my phone at the bystanders congregating around the yellow *Do Not Cross* tape. I zoom in and take a close-up shot of each one.

2

I stay at the crime scene for a while, interviewing the bystanders, watching all of the data collection and trying to figure out where to go from here. With any dead body, the first thing to do is to identify her.

We have to know who she is, what she was doing here, and who her family is in order to start to put together answers to all of the different questions. Until DNA is collected and the media is alerted, very little can be done. In this case, the media doesn't have to be notified. A few news vans arrive and I start to give them the basic rundown of what we have.

It's well into the evening by the time everything is done and after a whole day of subsisting on crackers and bad coffee, I yearn for a warm meal and a shower. My phone vibrates in my back pocket.

“Hey, do you mind if we cancel tonight?” I ask.

“Yes," Sydney replies in her wry, no-nonsense voice.

"I'm really beat. It's been a long day."

“Oh, come on," she pleads. “It will be fun. Just two drinks.”

I shake my head no, but I say yes. I always say yes to her. Sydney and I have been friends for a couple of years and we clicked right from the beginning. There are not that many people in the Los Angeles Police Department who I can say that about.

I meet her at our usual hangout, a dark, dingy bar not far from the police station on Wilcox Avenue. This place is typically frequented by cops in between shifts. It’s a place to blow off some steam before going home to their families.

Our jobs are stressful, but not in the usual way. Your adrenaline isn't pumping all day long; instead, there's this low-level feeling of anxiety that courses through every hour of every day. This is especially true for deputies on patrol.

Since I’ve become a detective, that feeling has somewhat moved into the background. My job now is to ask questions. Talk to people. Make them comfortable with me so that they will open up.

Frankly, I like it a lot more than what I used to do: driving around in a patrol car, pulling people over for speeding or blowing through red lights. You never knew who you were going to encounter or what was going to happen. Most of the time it was angry people running late to work but, on occasion, it was someone with fifty pounds of methamphetamines or a bag full of assault rifles in their trunk and no interest in getting arrested.

I arrive at the Tavern, with its warm wooden floors and soothing dark walls, and spot Sydney sitting at the bar on the far end. It's in the middle of a shift change so this place is not exactly full. That's just the way I like it.

Sydney has short dark hair and wide-set almond eyes, a perfect complement to her olive skin. She studied psychology at UCLA and got her Master's in criminal science. Then she went to the police academy. It's not exactly the most conventional path to becoming a cop, but then again, she's not exactly the most conventional girl.

Sydney has two sleeves of tattoos representing all of the most meaningful things in her life: favorite trips, inspiring quotes, and beloved pets. When she reaches over to get the bartender's attention, I glance at the one at the nape of her neck. A tall, elegant palm tree stands swaying in the wind, reaching up to her hairline. Sydney is originally from Minnesota and that palm tree represents her new life here in this land of sea and sand and a goodbye to her life back home.

My martini is ready just as I sit down.

“A girl could get used to this kind of service,” I joke and she laughs, tossing her hair from one side to the other.

“Why do we keep coming here?” I ask. "Aren't there any non-cop bars around?”

She puts her arms around me and gives me a kiss on the cheek.

“He's not coming here tonight.”

I roll my eyes and say, “I'm not talking about him.”

“Yes, you are,” she challenges me. "You love the Tavern. Why would you suddenly want to go to a new place?”

"I'm just sick of… cops. I think I need to get some new friends.”

“You can try, but I'm not sure that anyone else will put up with your crazy hours.”

“What are you talking about?” I gasp demonstratively.

"You’re unreliable. You’re always late. Sometimes you don't show up at all.”

"Is it my fault that I'm on call? It's not like I can say, 'hey, why don't you kill that guy at noon, because I have plans tonight?'"

"Man, wouldn't that be nice?" Sydney ponders and we both giggle.

I take a sip of my martini and look around again. Even though she is certain that Thomas Abrams won't show up tonight, I'm not so sure.

I keep turning on my stool and glancing over at the door. It hasn't been that long since our breakup. He works in my precinct and I've done a pretty good job avoiding him at work. The few times we've spoken, it has been all business, but you can't exactly do that in a place like this.

The Tavern is small. I'd be surprised if more than fifty people fit in this place. The ceilings are low and the bar top is tall. There are not enough stools and most of the time, we all huddle around each other. This probably wouldn't work in many other places, but the clientele here spends twelve hours a day in a car, so standing is a nice reprieve.

I ask Sydney about her day and she is excited to report that it was rather uneventful. Sometimes it's nice to have days like that. Even weeks. They make up for the flurry of activity that accompanies the rest of the time.

When we order a second round of drinks, I tell her that this is my last one and that I have come to a decision.

Inhaling the last of her beer by tipping her head and placing the glass at an almost ninety-degree angle, she asks, “That decision is?”

“I'm not dating any more cops.”

She laughs.

"I'm serious," I insist, secretly wondering if this decision is just like the one I had made earlier where I promised myself to run three miles a day. It's a lofty goal, but so far all I could manage was two miles, walking about half of the distance.

“So, who are you going to date then?”

A tall guy with piercing green eyes and a strong jaw walks up to us. He bends down and gives Sydney a kiss on the cheek.

"Hey there.” She whips around and kisses him on the mouth. Draping his arm around her shoulder, Patrick Flannery orders a beer.

They have been together for almost a year and just recently got engaged. Their wedding will be next June and I have already been pressed into service as the maid of honor.

"You two need to get a room,” I say, my voice tense with jealousy.

“We will, right after I finish this beer," Patrick says.

Sydney nudges him as if she's embarrassed, but we all know that nothing could be further from the truth. Playing with his tie, she twirls the end around her finger.

“Hey, be careful there or I'll have to iron this thing again.”

"I can do it for you.”

"Not in a million years. Have you seen this girl with an iron?” he asks me.

“Listen, can we just all agree that the most important thing that the academy taught us is how to iron the perfect crease?” Sydney asks.

“Probably second only to how to apprehend criminals,” I say.

“You two just don’t get it,” Patrick says as Sydney and I laugh. He is the type of guy who is very picky about his clothes and likes everything his way.

He straightens his tie and we continue to joke around. Unlike the majority of us, Patrick isn’t employed by the LAPD or the sheriff’s department. He works in communications at the FBI.

A call came in two years ago for a welfare check and Sydney was the one assigned to it. A wife had gone missing and her ex-husband had no idea where she'd gone.

Nothing seemed suspicious at first. Nice neighborhood. Nice husband. Appropriate emotions of concern.

When they tried to bring him in for more questioning, he went on the run, running down one of the neighbors in the process. They caught him and found three hundred pounds of explosives in the back of his car. The FBI was called in and Patrick was one of the people involved in speaking with the media. That's how they met. He took Sydney's statement and then asked her out for dinner. They spent the night together and they haven't been apart since.

I know that I said that I was going to go home soon, but after a few drinks, I find myself lingering even after Sydney and Patrick leave.

I don't know what I'm doing here. Am I seriously waiting for Thomas to show up? Why?

I can do so much better. I know that of course, but with the alcohol coursing through my veins, I can't help but miss him.

"Is this seat taken?" someone asks, sliding onto the stool next to me without waiting for my answer.

I spin around to face him, leaning against the back of the stool.

"Can I buy you another drink?" he asks, pointing to my empty glass and then holding up two fingers to the bartender.

"Are you in the habit of asking questions that you don't want answers to?" I challenge him, narrowing my eyes.

"Sometimes, when it feels right," he says, leaning closer. He runs his finger along his strong jawline and, for a moment, I lose myself in his sparkling blue eyes.

"Are you a body language expert then?" I ask, propping my head up with my hand and staring at his thick lashes. Those can't be real, right?

The bartender, a fast-moving spry woman with the no-nonsense look of an experienced teacher, brings us two martinis.

"You a big martini drinker?" I ask, looking him up and down.

Black leather jacket. Black slacks. Black shoes. The charcoal button-down shirt is open at the top.
No tie.

"Sometimes," he says.

When I don't move or say anything else, he raises his glass.

"Can I propose a toast?"

"No," I say, shaking my head, smiling just at the corner of my lips.

I want to deny it and I want to fight against it, but I like this. I like this dance, this tango, this back-and-forth. I like being wooed.

"I promised myself that I would only have two drinks and I already had them," I explain just as the expression on his face starts to fall. "If you had waited for my answer, then you wouldn't be out fifteen dollars."

"Eh," he waves, "it's a small price to pay to talk to a woman like you."

Woman.

I like that he referred to me as a woman instead of a girl.

It's not that the term girl is offensive. In most cases, it's not. It's just minimizing and, in a place like this, in this job, it's important that I don't allow myself to be minimized any more than I already am.

"I'm Luke," he says, extending his hand.

No more lines. No more jokes. No more playing around.

Suddenly, I have an inexplicable urge to kiss him. I practically have to purse my lips together to stop myself from just reaching over and grabbing him by the back of his neck and pulling him closer to me.

“I'm Kaitlyn," I say, shaking his hand.

His grip is strong, but there is no posturing.

It's not overtly and comically powerful, the way that some cops’ handshakes are in an effort to encapsulate their entire ego into that one squeeze.

Luke finishes his martini and leans so close to me that I can smell the vodka on his breath. I glance down at his mouth and watch as he slowly moves his tongue over his lower lip. When he looks up, his eyes practically imprint on mine.

"Do you want to get out of here?” he asks and I can't say no.

3

I follow him outside. I'd be lying if I said that it's against my better judgement. It's not.

He's cute and he's not a cop. I did say that I wasn't going to sleep with any more cops, right?

He grabs my hand right outside the bar and pulls me underneath his arm and gives me a tight squeeze. At first, this simple act catches me by surprise, but I don't pull away.

I look up at him, his arm still draped over my shoulder, and our lips touch. Did I kiss him or did he kiss me? I can't tell who made the first move, all that I know is that I need this moment to last as long as possible.

Our cars are parked in the lot around the corner. The small lot near the Tavern was packed as always and I had to find a spot on one of the side streets, after scanning a complicated No Parking sign to make sure that I didn't get towed.

When I click the button to unlock my car, Luke puts his arm around me and presses me against the door. He kisses me again. His hands make their way liberally around my body, eventually landing on my neck.

When I kiss him back, he mumbles, "Your place or mine?"

I try to pull away, but I can't force myself to stop.

"I live just a few blocks away," he says and kisses me again.

He wants me to leave my car here, but then I would need a ride back and suddenly, it's all becoming very logistically complicated.

"No, I'll drive," I say.

I wait for him to argue but he doesn't. I like that. He doesn't argue over things that don't matter.

I climb into my 2015 Toyota Prius, the car that I have just finished making payments on, and drive a few streets following his Honda CRV. He wasn't lying when he said he lived close. It's barely four streets away.

"Why didn't you just walk?" I ask, getting out of my car.

"I was driving home and saw the parking spot. I was just going to pop in and say hi to a few people, but then I saw you sitting at the bar and I had to know your name."

I roll my eyes.

He pulls me into his arms.

"Does that line work on every girl you bring home?" I ask, folding my arms across my chest and pressing the lock button in a demonstrative fashion, almost as if to punctuate the question.

"Yeah, I would have to say it has worked a few times." Luke smiles and a dimple forms in the middle of his cheek.

When he takes a small step closer to me, I can smell the breath mint that he had just popped into his mouth. I stare into his eyes and wait for him to make the first move, but he just lets his arms relax by his sides and waits.

I reach up and press my mouth to his. His lips are soft but strong, confident. Instead of rushing to get to the naked part, he takes his time and enjoys the moment. Then he pulls away, grabs my hand, and leads me to his apartment.

It's located on the second floor and the front door goes straight inside.

An older woman in a nightgown sits in a flimsy chair right in front of her open window, next to his front door.

“Hello, Mrs. Yandoli,” Luke says, holding my hand and giving me a little squeeze. “How are you tonight?”

"The heater isn’t working again,” she mutters, picking at her stringy hair that’s pulled into a tight bun on top of her head.

“Give me the name of the guy and I'll give him a call for you.”

“I already did. They were supposed to come today, but no one showed up.”

It's dark and the open hallway is poorly lit. Then something catches my eye and I see an outline of something underneath her nose. It takes me a moment to realize what I’m looking at, an oxygen tube. Mrs. Yandoli finishes one cigarette and immediately lights another, before turning around in her squeaky chair and grabbing the handle of the tank to roll it a little bit closer to her.

"How about this?” Luke suggests. “I look around for someone and I'll give them a call for you. I'll do it first thing in the morning.”

“Really?” Her eyes light up. “I'd really appreciate it.”

“Of course.”

“Thank you so much."

Luke unlocks his door, grabs my hand, and pulls me inside.

He kisses me again. Hard. He presses me against the wall and I kiss him back, burying my hands in his thick dark hair.

He tugs at my jacket and pulls it off of me. Then he slides his hand under my shirt. I continue to kiss him, but he senses that something is off.

“What's wrong?” Luke asks, keeping his mouth on mine.

“Nothing,” I mumble and kiss him again.

We make our way down the hallway to his bedroom. It's dark and the room is a kaleidoscope of shadows.

Somewhere behind me I find the bed. He lowers his body on top of me, pushing me down, and then… It becomes too much. I push against him. When he doesn't stop, I push him harder.

“No, no, no." Each word gets louder and louder.

“What's wrong?" he asks, his eyes big like saucers, surprise painted on his face.

"I can’t." I sit up and fold myself in half, burying my face in my knees.

I hate the darkness that engulfs me. I hate the anger that's boiling within me. I hate the fact that the only thing that I can think of is Thomas and what he did.

"Are you okay?" Luke reaches over and puts his hand softly on my shoulder. He barely touches me, but I shrug him off.

“I'm sorry. I thought that I could do this,” I say, standing up on my feet, realizing how shaky I am on them.

“What's going on?"

I swallow hard. Our eyes meet. Men in law enforcement tend to keep their hair cropped short at first. Very short. As the years go by, sometimes that changes. Not for all, but for some. Luke's hairstyle has a bit of arrogance to it or is it just confidence?

"I can't do this,” I say. “I'm going through something right now and I'm sorry that I wasted your time.”

I start to walk away and he flips on the light. It blinds me for a moment and then makes me see stars. I continue to walk away and he grabs my hand. I look at it and he lets me go.

"We don't have to do anything," Luke says, turning on the lights in the hallway while walking over to the teardrop lamp in the living room and flipping on that one as well.

“I know. That's why I’m leaving."

"No, that’s not what I meant. There’s no pressure to do anything. I just want to spend time with you.”

"Listen, you didn't do anything wrong. I'm just going through some stuff. A bad breakup and a whole lot of other things. I like you and I wanted this to happen, but I just can't. I'm not ready.”

That's as simple as I can put it and if he asks me again, I'm not going to be as nice. I wait, but he doesn't.

"Can I please give you my number?" Luke asks, but I reach for the door handle.

I turn around. The living room has a midcentury modern couch, charcoal with silver legs. It's a sleek design, just like the rest of the room. There’s a large fiddle-leaf fig with wide green leaves in the far corner of the room. The place looks like it has been staged by a West Elm decorator.

“Your apartment is really nice,” I say.

He nods thank you and I add, “I don't say that often.”

We share a moment of silence. It's quiet and comfortable, yet another surprising thing about being with him.

"Want to stay for coffee?" Luke asks.

I narrow my eyes. I'm sure that having coffee with a girl who just pushed him off of her is the last thing that he wants to do, but everything about his demeanor and the expression on his face tells me the opposite.

I'm about to say no, but the word, "Sure," escapes my lips instead.

He smiles at the corner of his lips and waves me over to follow him to the kitchen. It's small and located to one side of the living room with a big corner view of the street below.

Unlike the rest of the place, it's not modern and it's not updated. The cabinets look like they're from the seventies, flat and without any personal touches. They have small round knobs in the corner of each and a few are splattered with the same matte white paint as the rest of the kitchen. The stove is clean but dated and matches the black of the microwave.

"How long have you lived here?" I ask when he makes a pot of coffee.

"A few years. Why?"

"Just wondering."

"I'm thinking of repainting this kitchen, but my landlord is an ass and won't let me take the cost out of the rent. I should move, but I work too many hours and I don't have the time or the energy."

"For what?"

"For everything. For anything. The time to look for a place, the time to pack up this one, the time to move. So, I just keep putting it off."

"I get it." I nod, thinking back to all of the clothes in the closet that I've been meaning to go through to donate to the Salvation Army. It's a project that I've had hanging over my head for months that I haven't gotten around to starting.

"It looks like this place is pretty affordable though," I say, trying to be delicate in my wording.

"Cheap, you mean? You'd be surprised. It's two grand a month, so not as affordable as one might think."

I nod in solidarity and say, "I have a one bedroom as well and I pay $1600, but the rent has been creeping up. I started out at $1400."

"I know that I should buy something, but with any decent condo or house going for half a million, I'd have to save at least seventy-five percent for the down payment."

"Yeah, I know what you mean." I nod.

"Besides, there's that whole other thing, you know."

I tilt my head and narrow my eyebrow.

"No, what do you mean?"

"I keep thinking that I might meet someone and then it would be nice to buy a place together. Have you ever lived with anyone?" he asks, pouring our coffees into two big mugs. His is from San Francisco and mine is from Wichita.

"Kansas?" I ask, lifting mine up.

"My family is from there. My mom sent it to me when I moved here."

"To answer your question," I say, inhaling the aroma and letting it seep into every part of me, "I was close to buying a condo with my ex, but things didn't exactly work out."

Suddenly, I start to feel very self-conscious. I run my finger over the rim of the mug and move my jaw from one side to the other.

"Aren't we supposed to be on our third or fifth or maybe thirtieth date before we start talking about our exes?"

"Yeah, something like that." He smiles and I laugh.

Luke shows me to the living room and I sit down next to him on the couch. There are enormous built-in bookshelves all across the opposite wall, engulfing the television.

"These are gorgeous," I say, resisting the urge to stand up and run my fingers over the books.

"Built them myself."

"You did? Where? How?"

"I like doing woodworking. It's relaxing. You need space though so I'm taking classes at this studio in Silver Lake. I should really get a house so that I can have a garage."

"That's awesome," I say.

"It would have been cheaper to buy them, but I liked making them."

"Crafted things are always more expensive in time and money."

Suddenly, the mood seems to shift. I look at the way the light falls on his face and the way his eyes twinkle when he talks. Then something comes over me. It has something to do with what he said, but I don't know exactly what. I lean a little bit closer to him and before he has the chance to move away, I kiss him.

He freezes for a moment and doesn't respond, but then he kisses me back, hard. He pulls away, only to take the cup out of my hand and place it on the coffee table before pushing me back against the couch. I feel the hardness of his body as he presses himself against me. We stay this way for a while, with our lips locked and our bodies intertwined.

Just as his hand starts to make its way up my shirt, my phone vibrates. When I pull it out of my back pocket to put it aside, I glance at the screen. I sit up to make sure that my eyes aren't deceiving me.

"I have to take this," I say.

Why is she calling at this hour? She never calls this late. She hardly ever calls after five p.m.

"Mom?"

"She's missing," she says. Her voice is frantic and out-of-control. I can hear her stumbling around her house, turning things over, as if she's looking for something small, easy to lose.

"Who? Who's missing?"

Something falls to the floor and makes a loud banging sound.

"Mom?" I hold the phone closer to my ear to make it easier to hear. "What's going on?"

"She's missing! Your sister is missing!"

4

My mom has a tendency to catastrophize. That's what the therapist at the department told me. She calls me once and if I'm busy and I don't respond then she calls again ten minutes later. When she calls for the third time, twenty minutes later, her energy level is through the stratosphere thinking that I must be injured or dead.

This didn't just start when I went to the academy. This has been going on my whole life. Everything is always a big deal. Everything is an emergency. Everything is an over-the-top catastrophe.

That's what makes me hesitate when she calls about Violet.

"Mom, she's probably just with a friend."

"No, no, no," Mom insists. I hate to admit it, but her worries feel different. Odd.

She’s scared, frantic, out-of-control just like always, but there's something else.

“Tell me what is going on. Calmly. Please.”

She takes a deep breath. I can almost hear her counting back from five, just like she told me she’d learned to do on a recent meditation app that she’d installed on her phone.

“Violet went out with friends. She was supposed to be back by nine. It's a school night. Her friend’s mom dropped her off at nine.”

“How do you know this?” I ask.

“I talked to her. Nancy said she dropped her off right in front of the house, but she never came in. She isn’t here. How can that be? How can she not be here?”

"I don't know," I say, muttering to myself. "She was dropped off, you know this for sure?”

“She went over to Kaylee’s house after school to work on a social studies project. They made the poster, whatever, hung out, and had dinner. Nancy made pasta and then that was it. She said she dropped her off right in front of the house.”

“Did she see her walk in?” I ask.

"I don't know,” Mom says after a long pause. “I guess not.”

My mom is quiet now, thinking. Her usual anxious energy starts to dissipate, almost as if it's being sucked out of her.

I try to think of all the possible things that could've happened. Violet is thirteen-years-old. She doesn't even have a bad relationship with my mom like I did at that age. She's a good girl. She follows the rules. She doesn't stay up late. Mom is always talking about what a great kid she is, silently comparing her to me at that age.

I try to think of what to do. This could be a mistake. Maybe she made plans to go out with someone else and will be back in a few hours. Maybe it's nothing. There's always that first time, right? That first time when a teenager does something out of character?

I also know that when my sister says she'll be somewhere, she's always there, on time. She's punctual to a fault.

I don't know what to do. I pace around the room holding the phone and asking my mom the same questions over and over again. She has few answers. She's getting frantic again and even though I tell her to calm down, I feel myself getting more and more upset with every passing minute.

Violet doesn't run away. That's completely out of the question. Violet goes to the library on Friday afternoons instead of going to parties. She stays there until closing when Mom picks her up. She's the complete opposite of who I was at her age and that's what's so scary. If this were me, I'd tell her to call my friends and then ask them for the names of the kids who she didn't know I was friends with.

What about my sister?

I wasn't a particularly outgoing kid, but I had a small group of acquaintances and I liked boys. I liked flirting with them and I liked the way that they looked at me. I liked kissing them.

I know that Violet likes boys, too, but if she wanted to meet up with one, why not tell Mom? She's particularly strict. She can't stay out all night, of course, but if she told her that she was going to stay at a friend's house, that would be okay, as long as she knew who the parents were.

"Did you have a fight?" I ask.

"No."

"Please tell me the truth. I need to know everything."

"No, we didn't."

"What about that art school she wanted to go to?"

There's a pause on the other line.

“Mom?” I ask. “Remember how you were arguing about it and she stayed with me? Any chance she ran away?”

“No, absolutely not. We haven’t talked about that for months. She was trying to prove to me that she’s going to follow the rules. She was doing everything right. Do you think I should call the police?”

The word police reverberates in my mind. It’s actually the Sheriff’s department, but I know what she means. I moved out at eighteen and I don’t know anyone there, professionally.

“Yes, of course,” I say.

“Really?” She gasps. It hits me that a part of her must’ve thought that she was blowing this out of proportion as much as I did. That is until I confirmed her worries.

"Maybe you should call?” Mom asks, her voice cracking.

“No, I don't live there. It's all secondhand information. They are going to want to talk to you anyway. You call and make a report. I'll be there as soon as I can.”

“You're coming up?”

“Of course.”

"Oh my God! This is serious. This is serious, right?" If I thought that my mom's voice was out of control before, I hadn't seen anything yet.

"Mom, it's going to be fine. I'm just coming up as a precaution," I say as an avalanche of sobs thunders through the phone.

"She's gone. She's gone!" she screeches, ignoring me.

I wish that there were something I could do to make her feel better. I have never been very good at consoling her. I have always found my mom difficult to deal with. She's highly emotional and, given the fact that I'm prone to anxiety, she's not exactly the most relaxing person to be around, but right now we have a problem to solve. I have a missing sister and I'm going to do everything in my power to find her.

"Mom, you have to calm down," I say sternly, lowering my voice an octave, just like I often do at work when I want to be taken seriously.

I'd noticed that a while back. Men tend to take it more seriously. Law enforcement officers from other departments tend to listen to me more intently. I don't make it comically low, just enough to exude authority to play to the unconscious biases of my listener.

“We're going to find Violet, I promise you. Everything's going to be fine,” I say confidently.

She’s immediately put at ease by my sternness and control of the situation. I'm glad that I can do that for her; now who's going to do that for me?

When I hang up, I look up at Luke.

“It’s going to be okay, you’ll find her,” he promises me and pulls me into his arms. “Get in touch if you need anything,” he says after we exchange numbers. "Now go and find her.”

I DRIVE to my apartment and throw some clothes into an overnight bag. I pack a few toiletries along with my chargers, my computer, and my iPad. Half an hour later, I'm driving down the empty freeway ten miles above the speed limit with my jaw clenched tight.

I put on one song after another, but nothing holds my attention. One is too upbeat, another is too depressing. Some are too popular, and others are just simply annoying. After a few more tries, I turn off the sound altogether and just listen to the steady lull of wheels grinding against asphalt.

I was so confident on the phone with my mom, but as the minutes tick by, my worries multiply. The truth is that I'm terrified. In my line of work,

I see the worst of humanity. People can be cruel, mean, and petty, but I also see the worst of what can happen even if there is no ill intent. Accidents happen all the time. Terrible tragedies that happen for no reason whatsoever.

I hold my breath and I hope that Violet isn't lost at all, but rather just not found. Maybe she went out with a friend, got drunk, and is now just sleeping it off. Teenagers do that all the time. It's stupid, inconsiderate, and selfish, but at least she will be fine in the morning, besides the hangover.

Maybe she is just hanging out with a guy she likes. Maybe she stayed out too late and is now afraid to come home. There're so many possibilities of what could have happened. The problem is that the more time that passes, the narrower those possibilities become.

If she comes back in the middle of the night, she just did something that teenagers do. What if she doesn't come back in the morning? She wouldn't stay out with a friend that late. She would never let Mom worry for so long. What could have happened then?

When I take the exit for 338, the highway that goes up to the mountain communities hovering above San Bernardino, I remember how frustrated I used to feel by my mom's worst-case scenario thinking.

I remember how if I were half an hour late getting back from my friend's house, she'd be pacing around the living room, anxious and on the verge of tears. In a time before text messaging, if I didn't answer my cell phone and tell her that I couldn't talk, she would keep calling me over and over again leaving messages. She'd make me so angry and once in a while, I wouldn't reply on purpose.

What if this is what Violet is doing?

What if this is why she disappeared?

I grip the steering wheel tighter.

Given my line of work, my mom's fears and the worst-case scenarios are very real outcomes for all of the victims and the families that I come in contact with. Growing up, I kept telling her how unlikely all of her thoughts of doom and gloom were, but now I deal with people who find themselves in these situations all the time.

It's January and though that doesn't mean much in Los Angeles or anywhere in Southern California because the days are still mostly sunny and the temperature stays at a cool 65°, here in the mountains, snow has settled in for the cold winter.

The drive usually takes around two and a half hours, but it just started snowing and the road is slick. The snow that fell about a week ago still lays thickly on the ponderosa pines.

The temperature is well below 30°. This has always been a special, unusual little ecosystem, hidden right below the clouds. The Hollywood Hills near Los Angeles aren't tall enough to stop the weather, but the San Bernardino Mountains are tall and jagged and the winters are harsh.

I've always loved skiing here because during the days it can be in the 60s and even warmer with the hot sun heating you up through the thin air. From December through March, heavy snowfall is not uncommon creating snowdrifts of four to five feet tall.

This is the place where I grew up. Up here, the communities are scattered, mainly focused around the lakes. The biggest one is Big Bear Lake, my hometown, but there's also Lake Arrowhead, and a smaller Green Valley Lake. There are other small towns like Running Springs and Crestline, which have a few thousand inhabitants each. Tourism is the main business. In the winters, people ski and snowboard. In the summers, they rent boats and water skis.

White flurries collide with my windshield and I know that my Prius is not the optimal vehicle for driving in the snow. I used to have a four-wheel-drive, but the gas was expensive and I needed to find bigger parking spots so I sold it and got this one. Whenever I come up here in the winter, I strongly regret that decision.

About five minutes away from Running Springs, the first town on the drive up the hill, I see the flashing signs telling me to put on chains.

"Perfect," I mutter to myself.

Chains are a good idea but an annoyance to deal with especially in the middle of the night. You have to pull over, get out of your vehicle, get them from the trunk, and then spend a few minutes wrapping them carefully around each wheel to make sure that you have a good grip on the road and don't slide around causing accidents.

After forgetting them once and then spending an hour standing in line at the general store to buy an expensive, overpriced new pair with the rest of the tourists, I carry them with me in the trunk at all times.

What I did forget was my gloves.

With the wind whizzing around my ears, I grip my frozen hands on the ice-cold metal and try to wrap the chains around the snow-covered tires, cursing myself. For a moment, I'm tempted by the bright lights of the exit sign pointing in the direction where I can buy another pair, but I grit my teeth and focus.

The cold nips at my nose and my cheeks, but I force myself to stay. Mom has plenty at home.

5

I get to my mom's house in Big Bear. It's an A-frame home that's a few streets away from the lake. My mom bought it back in the '70s and refused to move when the prices started to go up.

Big Bear is mainly a vacation market type of place. Tourists everywhere. A lot of people from LA have moved out here and others bought second homes when they were still affordable. Now, one goes for almost half a million if you want to get a three-bedroom, two-bath in a good area, that is. Second homes used to be something that people enjoyed on weekends, but now they are mainly rented out as an Airbnb.

My mom's house, my old house, is a three-bedroom, one-bath, and less than 1200 square feet. That's considered quite small, as they build much bigger now. It has low ceilings and a tight dark kitchen. It has shag carpeting and a big fireplace that my mom orders wood for every winter.

A lot of my friends that I grew up with moved down to Southern California to get away from the snow, but those who are ski bums and the like have stayed behind. My mom never asked me to stay, she knew that I wouldn't. I like skiing and I snowboard pretty well, but there's no way that I could stay here for long.

When I finally get home, I find my mom walking back and forth around the living room, completely distraught. Her eyes are bloodshot. Her pale skin is practically translucent, so gray that it's practically green. The lighting in this place isn't the best and there are dark shadows everywhere. She likes it this way. It looks like it's twilight at all times.

I've bought my mom a number of lamps over the years, but they just end up going into the makeshift garage that's really a big storage unit where she keeps everything that has been discarded but she can't bring herself to throw away.

Her hair is curly and big around her head like always, but a little bit messier and I can tell that she's been pulling at it, something of a tendency of hers. I walk through the door without knocking and she grabs me immediately and takes me into her arms.

"I'm so glad you're here," she whispers my name over and over again. Her voice cracks practically at each syllable. "She's just gone. I can't believe that she left."

She smells of cinnamon and mint mixed with chocolate. I know that she's been eating her favorite Andes candies and she always lights that cinnamon candle from Bath and Body Works. I have bought her more than one on occasion and she always burns it down to the very end, keeping the glass containers in a collection on her dresser.

The toilet flushes and a police officer comes out from the back. I wonder if he had noticed the carpet around the toilet that has been there since I was a kid and whether he, like everyone else in the modern world, was disgusted by it. Another thing my mom refuses to change.

"This is," my mom starts to introduce him, but he extends his hand and says, "I'm Deputy Tourney… Greg Tourney."

He's a tall, masculine man who looks like he walked out of a 1960s police drama with everything, including the mustache. He looks to be in his 40s but is fit with piercing blue eyes that catch me off guard at first. From the outside, he's quite attractive, but there's something off about him.

I tell him who I am and can't help but flash my detective badge from the LAPD. As soon as he sees it, his temper and everything about his demeanor changes. It's like there's a shift. Suddenly, he's not so friendly or outgoing anymore. A tension appears. It's like when, back in school, the teacher would ask you to read out loud and you knew that you were going to mess up just because you were doing it in front of the whole class.

"I'm just here because she's my mom," I explain, trying to put him at ease. "I'm not here in any sort of official capacity."

"Yes, of course. I understand," he says, but I don't believe him.

I decide to tread lightly. I put my bag down in the living room and we all sit down around the weathered coffee table, with the edges rounded by age rather than by design, to talk about my sister. To say that this is surreal would be a huge understatement.

Tourney takes notes. I see his little notebook and my mom repeats the story. It's pretty much verbatim to what she told me earlier on the phone. He then turns his attention to me. He asks me when the last time was I spoke to her. I try to think of when and I can't. I look at my phone.

“I guess it has been a week. I thought that we had texted, but I was kind of busy. I have a few cases that have piled up on me.”

“Uh-huh,” he mumbles and licks the tip of his pen before pressing it against the paper.

I glance over at my mom. I'm glad she called the cops. I told her to do that, but I wasn't sure if she would. Sometimes she takes things into her own hands, but sometimes she tends to waver and wait for me to fix her problems.

She was a young mom with me and the whole time that I was growing up, she sort of relied on me to help her along in life. I didn't realize that until I got older and now I find it a little difficult to deal with.

Growing up, of course, it was just natural. I had no idea that there were other mothers around, but now that I'm older, I know that I would never want to be a mom like that. That's probably why I haven't had kids yet. I just never think that I'm ready for it.

An older man who looks and acts like Tourney’s boss comes in to talk to us. Captain Talarico is a few years older, but much quicker on his toes. There are lines that have settled into his face and a haircut that doesn't seem exactly straight across, but I get a completely different feel from him.

"We'll get right on this. Everyone in the department will be on the lookout for your daughter now," he says.

His confidence puts me a little bit more at ease.

They ask a few more questions and then they take off. They say that they'll be in touch soon, probably in a few hours if they hear anything. They seem optimistic and I like that, but I know as well as anybody that these cases have to be solved really quickly and these girls have to be found within a few hours if we want to get them back alive and in one piece.

After the cops leave, my mom heads into the yellow-wallpapered kitchen and opens the refrigerator. This is her go-to move when she's nervous. She opens it up and looks inside, bending in half to peer into its depths. The problem is that there isn't much there.

She's not much of a cook and neither am I. Growing up, we generally ordered takeout or ate leftovers. Sometimes I heated up macaroni and cheese and occasionally, she made eggs and other easy dishes. When I was fifteen, she learned how to make casseroles so we had that for nearly a year until we both wanted to throw up.

My mom is thin and trim, and she likes to wear UGGs around the house to keep warm. The heater has been acting up and the only source that has been working is the fireplace, which requires constant tending. They are real logs and it's a real fire after all.

"I can't believe that it's still so cold here," I say when she closes the refrigerator door, pulling out some packaged frozen food from the freezer. She holds two packages up, one in each hand.

One is some sort of Indian dish and another is Italian.

“Want to share?" she asks.

"Sure. Let's go with Palak Paneer."

She smiles.

I know that's her favorite as well. She gets it down the hill at the local Trader Joe’s. I would be lying if I said that I didn't basically survive on that back at my place.

I decide to reheat it in the microwave since the stove is too daunting right now. We sit down around the small kitchen island and wolf it all down without saying a word.

I look out the window at the enormous pine tree, past the houses across the street at the whitening sky. It's almost morning now, daylight is just filtering through the night. Sunrises have always been magnificent around here, full of reds and yellows, lighting up the sky. Today, I don't want sunrise to come. I don't want time to pass because I know what that means.

"Is there any chance that she could just be at her friend's house and maybe fell asleep or something like that?"

"No, I told you." She shakes her head. "Nancy dropped her off already and she was supposed to come inside."

"I know, but what if she went somewhere else? What if she had a guy meet her and they went out? What if it's not a big deal at all?" I ask, keenly aware of the desperation in my voice.

"Yeah, I guess, but she's not you. She's your sister and we both know that she doesn't do stuff like that." My mom's voice is resigned, no longer frantic and out of control, just tired and lost in thought.

I'm not sure what to do now. I mean, of course I do know the proper steps to take as an investigator, but at this moment, I don't know how to console her. I don't know how to make her feel better any more than I know how to make myself feel better. I just wish that I didn't know all the things that I know about what might have happened to her.

Unfortunately, I do.

6

An hour later I get back in my car, this time wearing a pair of warm gloves and a hat that I haven't seen since I was ten years old and head over to Nancy Dillinger's house. That's out in Fawnskin, about twenty minutes away.

Nancy is Kaylee's mom and Kaylee is Violet's friend, the one who supposedly dropped her off. My mom talked to her already and she doesn't want to come with me.

I don't blame her, but I have to. This is why I'm here. This is what I need to do. It's barely seven o'clock in the morning as I make my way around the lake. Snow has been plowed and piled up high along the pine trees. The streets are relatively empty, just a few commuters here and there going where they need to go.

People come here to see the winter wonderland and that's exactly what it is, the morning after a blizzard. The flurries stopped coming just as I got to my house and they are just settling into place. It's supposed to stay relatively cool today, but by tomorrow, the sun will undoubtably melt them into slush.

Nancy and Kaylee live past the boulders up on the other side of the lake in a small cabin that requires me to drive up an almost vertical incline. When I park, I immediately put on the emergency brake. I've heard that the internet in these parts isn't that great, but I guess this view more than makes up for it. I look out at the lake, surrounded by tall pines and partially covered fresh snow glistens below.

When I knock on Nancy's door, it takes her a bit to answer. I texted her earlier, but I got no response and decided to come anyway.

She appears at the door, bleary-eyed, dressed in a thick bathrobe with her hair pinned up into curlers. I haven't seen anyone sleep in curlers since I don't know when. I used to watch a lot of sitcoms from the sixties when I was a kid and I guess that's probably the last time that I've seen this kind of look. I had no idea anyone still did it.

Nancy rubs her eyes and covers her brows with her hand to look at me more carefully.

"I'm sorry to bother you, but I'm Kaitlyn Carr, Violet's sister. I'm a detective with the LAPD and my mom told me that she was missing. So, I came up here to try to find her."

Nancy nods, but offers me nothing.

I continue anyway with, "I just wanted to hear what happened from you directly. You dropped her off?"

"Is this why you're bothering me this early in the morning?"

"I'm sorry that I'm here, but my sister's missing and every minute is important. We need to find some leads as to where she might've gone."

Nancy shakes her head and says, "I already told your mom everything I know."

"I understand, but I really want to hear it from you."

Her voice is coarse like she has been a smoker for over forty years. She tightens her belt and doesn't invite me inside. I wish I had worn a warmer coat, but this one will just have to do.

"What do you want to know?" she asks, pulling a pack of cigarettes from her plush pocket with a coffee cup on the front and lighting it with the lighter in her other hand.

The tips of her fingers are so white. They're practically blue and her nails are painted green but peeling in parts. She holds her cigarette with her fingertips and inhales deeply, sucking in every last drop of nicotine.

“So, Violet was here with you last night?"

"Yes, with Kaylee. They played all evening and then I drove her home."

"What time was that?"

"I don't know, 9:00? I dropped her off and I saw her walking toward the house."

"Did you see her walk into the house?" I ask, folding my hands across my chest to stay warm.

"No, we turned around and drove away. I mean maybe, but I don't remember the door opening or not."

I have no idea if this is her usual demeanor, cool, defensive, and distant, or if she’s trying to hide something.

That's the thing that you have to figure out as a detective; is this person you're interviewing naturally hostile and evasive or are they acting like this because they’ve done something wrong? It's not as easy to figure that out as television shows would have you believe.

I peer into Nancy's house and see that it has similar shag carpeting to what my mom has at her house, only hers is green.

I see the whole living room from the front door, as well as a small bathroom to the side and another room going up the stairs. The house can't be more than one bedroom.

"Do you two share a room?" I ask, wondering where Kaylee sleeps.

"The bedroom upstairs has a walk-in closet. She has her bed there. Why?" she snaps.

"You have a really nice view from here," I say.

"Is that why you're here? To talk about my house?"

"No, not at all. I was just making a comment."

"Well, I could be sleeping right now and so I would think that you would at least not waste my time."

"Okay, I apologize," I say in my best detective voice, stern and no longer very friendly.

If she doesn't want to chitchat, then that's absolutely fine with me. I'm not a fan in the first place.

"So, you saw my sister walking up to the house?" I ask.

"Yes."

"Did she walk across the grass or did you drop her off near the driveway?"

She looks at me and then shakes her head. "Why does that matter?"

"I'm just trying to get a clear picture here."

"You're wasting time. You, yourself, said that time is of the essence and yet you're here asking me these dumb questions."

"Okay, Mrs..."

Suddenly I forgot her name.

She waits for me to say something and then volunteers it, even more annoyed that she was before.

"Would you mind if I talk to your daughter? Maybe she would have some ideas. Maybe she would know if Violet had some plans to meet up with someone else after you dropped her off."

"Sure. Be my guest," Nancy says, surprising me.

She puts out the cigarette on the ashtray, strategically positioned right outside the house on the deck and waves me inside. The living room is even smaller than it seemed on the outside. The kitchen is an open concept and there are probably two cabinets along with an apartment-size stove and a college style mini fridge. I wonder how long she has been living here, but I don't want to ask any extraneous questions and possibly get on her bad side. She calls her daughter by yelling up the stairs.

"Okay, I'll be right there," Kaylee mumbles from upstairs.

Five minutes later, while I take a seat on the small leather sofa, she comes downstairs. She's still wearing last night's makeup and her hair is lopsided and messed up as if she had slept on it wet.

Dressed in an oversized t-shirt with a unicorn on it and loose-fitting pajama pants, she pulls a sweatshirt over her head and waves hello.

When I introduce myself, she gives me a slight nod, taking a seat to the left of me. It's kind of a makeshift sitting area made of crates and a pillow.

"I'm really sorry about Violet," she says with a shrug.

"Yes, me, too. That's why I'm here."

"She still hasn't come home?"

"No."

Nancy makes some coffee behind us and I expect her to offer us some, but she doesn't. Instead, she pours herself a cup and my mouth waters as I smell the aroma.

“So, you haven't talked to her since last night?"

"No," Kaylee says with a shrug. "She was here all evening. We were working on a civil war project and then she... Then my mom dropped her off."

"Is there a reason why she did that? Was my mom busy?"

"Yeah, I guess so. I'm not really sure."

"Does my mom usually pick her up?"

"I think she said something about your mom not wanting to drive all the way out here at night and Mom doesn't mind. Sometimes we stop in and do our grocery shopping at that time, when the stores are emptier."

"That makes sense."

A lot of locals do that in the winter since both stores tend to be overrun by tourists on their ski trips. It can sometimes take an hour to get through the lines.

Kaylee pushes her dishwater-blonde hair behind one ear straightening the messy part on the other side. When she realizes that it won't behave, she tucks it all into a loose bun using the scrunchie on her wrist.

"So, after you dropped her off, what then?" I ask.

"I don't know. She was supposed to go inside and that's it."

"She wasn't going to go out with anyone after that, like maybe a guy who she'd arranged to meet up with?"

She shakes her head.

"Kaylee, you're not going to get in trouble," I say, reaching over and touching her hand, but she pulls away from me. "I'm just really trying to find out what happened to her and Violet is not going to get in trouble either. I'm just really worried about my sister."

Kaylee shakes her head. She holds eye contact with me pretty easily. She's either a marvelous liar or she's telling the truth. I can't tell which one quite yet.

"I didn't see her walk up to the door. Mom just turned around and we drove away, but she must have, right?"

"I would think so, but she didn't come home."

"Do you think something bad happened to her?" Kaylee asks, putting her hand over her mouth.

"I really hope not."

I wait for her to add something.

“Is there anything else?” she asks instead.

I shake my head.

No one says anything for a while and then I lean so close to her, I can smell her breath. She hasn't had the chance to brush her teeth yet and I get the scent of Cheetos and Dr. Pepper, but no alcohol.

”Kaylee," I say, reaching over to her again and taking her hand in mine. "Kaylee, I want you to know how serious this is. If you know anything, if she said anything off the cuff or was acting strange. Please, you have to tell me. Any little detail can help."

Kaylee shakes her head, looking straight into my eyes. She lifts up her shoulders and flounces a bit, but she doesn't pull her hands away. She just lets it rest there.

"I really wish that there was something I could help you with, but I have no idea. I can't imagine her wanting to meet up with a guy and not telling me about it though."

“Neither can I,” I say silently to myself.

"Is there anyone that she liked at school? Is there another friend that she might have wanted to go out with?"

She thinks about it for a moment, but then shakes her head.

"She used to like this guy named Neil Goss, but he was kind of mean to her in math class and so that was that, but that's all I can think of."

I write down the name, using the Note app on my phone. I show her the screen and she confirms the spelling.

"He's in your grade?"

"Yes. He lives over in Big Bear Lake in a big house. A mansion, really. His dad is an attorney. Everyone has a crush on him at some point."

"What do you mean by that?"

"Oh, you know the type, cocky, confident, good at sports, really easy on the eyes. I liked him back in fifth grade, but then I found out that he's a dick."

"Violet? She liked him, too?"

"Big crush, major one, but he has a girlfriend, Natalie D'Achille. She's also popular. She's part of a twin set."

"Twins?" I ask.

"Actually triplets," she corrects herself. "She has two brothers, not identical. They've all been pretty popular ever since elementary school and Natalie and Neil have been on and off for about two or three years now. Recently they've been on."

"What happened between Neil and Violet?"

"I'm not sure exactly. They worked on some project together and then he started to ignore her. She thought maybe that he would like her but then… I don't know exactly what happened."

I nod my head, taking it all in. The drama of middle school is difficult to track, but in this case, it's the only lead I have. Well, besides going to the neighbors and seeing if they have any recordings from their Nest cameras to see what actually happened last night.

Kaylee pulls out her phone and offers to give me Neil's phone number. A wave of excitement rushes through me as I put the number into my contact list.

"I didn't realize you had it," I say.

"Yeah. We all kind of stay in touch. We have this big group text, but he doesn't always reply. Sometimes he posts stuff on TikTok and Instagram."

I write down all of his social media info along with his address that she finds for me in the school's directory.

"Thank you so much," I tell her after I collect all of that information. "I hope it's nothing, but I'll let you know. I hope she comes back later this morning with a big smile on her face, but we have to take action now just in case, you understand?"

"Yes, of course." Kaylee nods, wrapping her hands around her knees. "I really hope you find her. I can't imagine that something might've happened."

I walk out of their house with shivers running down my spine, the way she said that, it took me by surprise. On one hand, it feels like she's just making a general comment about her missing friend.

On the other hand, something feels off, like, is she telling me everything?

Does she know anything?

I look at the time and it's not even eight. I decide to stop at the Starbucks before heading over to Neil's house.

I text my mom to find out if she has any more news on Violet, but she doesn't. After ordering a latte and warming up in my car. I drive over to the Whispering Pines area near the lake, famous for its grand mansions, some of which are ten thousand square feet.

My GPS takes me right over to one with enormous columns and an elaborately carved wooden gate up front. I press the button on the intercom and wait.

No one answers. I push it again.

"Hello?" A faint female voice comes on.

"My name is Kaitlyn Carr. I'm a detective with the LAPD and I would like to talk to Neil Goss, please."

The person on the other end doesn't respond right away.

Then I hear her say, "Timothy," in barely a whisper.

"Thomas, there's a detective here who wants to talk to Neil," she whimpers, keeping her finger on the talk button, allowing me to hear. A few minutes later, the gate swings open and I drive in.

7

Mrs. Michelle Goss is a thin woman with a nervous energy. She has a string of pearls around her neck and her hair is wet and piled loosely on top of her head.

Her skin is almost translucent and when she opens the door, she leans out keeping it tightly closed around her as if to prevent me from looking inside.

I introduce myself again, extending my hand. She pushes hers out through the thin slit in the doorway and shakes it.

"Can I come in? I have something to talk to you about," I say boldly.

"Yes, of course," she says, hesitating.

She doesn't want to let me in, but she can't come up with a good excuse to turn me away. When I walk in, an enormous staircase greets me and pulls my eyes up to the cathedral-like ceilings. The wide spectacle of a crystal chandelier hangs sparkling above our heads.

"You are Mrs. Goss?" I ask.

"Yes, of course. I'm sorry, I should have introduced myself," she says, holding her hand tightly around her neck as if she needs it to be there to keep her bathrobe closed.

"I'm really sorry to bother you and I know that it's really early," I say, "but it couldn't wait."

"What, exactly?" she asks, tucking her other hand into her plush pockets.

I hesitate. I don't know how to put it exactly.

Should I mention that my sister's missing or should I ask her about her son first? Better yet, should I just ask to talk directly to him?

"Do you think that I can speak to your son, Neil?"

"Why?" she snaps.

"Okay, bad decision," I say to myself.

"Mrs. Goss, can I call you Michelle?"

"No, you may not.” She shakes her head, straightening her back. Perhaps she’s not as much of a pushover as she seems.

"As I've said earlier, I'm a detective with the LAPD, but I'm not here in any official business,” I start, softening my approach and trying to appeal to her as a victim. “I grew up here and my sister is in Neil's class. I believe they have math together. I really need to talk to him. She's been missing since last night and we can't find her anywhere."

Suddenly, her demeanor changes as if it were on a switch. The tension in her face dissipates, her shoulders slope down, and her lip's soften.

She pulls her hands out of her pockets and leads me to the dining room table so that we can both sit down.

"Would you like to have some coffee, tea, breakfast?"

"No, I don't have time. I just would really like to speak to your son. As you can imagine, I'm really worried about my sister."

"Yes, of course," Mrs. Goss says and heads toward the staircase. "I'll get him right now."

She leaves me alone to look around.

I have been in plenty of big mansions and estates in my capacity as a detective interviewing witnesses and victims, but this is different.

First of all, it has an unusual German style, white and black paneling, but done very tastefully. The windows have big lattices across them. There's an alcove near the dining room table and I walk over there to look out onto the street below.

There's so much shrubbery and landscaping that you wouldn't even know that there is a neighbor right next door. I make my way out to the foyer and admire the parquet floors and the modern art hanging on the walls.

You wouldn't think that it would fit this kind of older style house, but somehow it does. I wonder if Mrs. Goss decorated this place herself or if she had any help. I know that I would need some. I think back to my own sad little fig leaf plant that I can barely keep alive and the few pictures on the wall that I got at Target. There's no way I could do a house like this.

A few minutes later, Neil comes downstairs. Shaggy blonde hair, pimply face but with the casual, confident bravado of a kid who runs the school.

I introduce myself and his mom hovers near him. I wish that she would leave, but I don't want to make her uncomfortable and make him stop talking to me.

"Can I ask you about my sister Violet?"

"Yes, of course," he says. "She's in my math class."

"What is your relationship with her?"

"I don't know," he says with a casual shrug. "We're friends, I guess, or maybe not."

"You don't know whether you are friends?"

"I don't know. It's complicated. I know her and we worked on some projects together, but that's about it. Why?"

"Well, she's missing." I hate the sound of that statement. It's so unresolved, tense, final.

"What do you mean missing?" he asks. He furrows his brows a little bit, but I can't exactly tell if he is surprised or just generally confused.

"She didn't come home last night," I explain. "She got dropped off, but she didn't go inside and we haven't seen her since. My mom called me and then called the cops. We're all looking for her."

"Is that why you're here?" he asks, leaning against the wall as if he doesn't have a worry in the world.

"Well, someone told me that you two might have had a thing and I just wanted to ask when was last time that you saw her?"

"You heard that we had a thing? What are you talking about?" he asks, clearly uncomfortable.

This is the first real reaction that I've had from him. I don't say anything but wait instead.

"No, absolutely not," he mutters.

"You never had any romantic interactions with her?" I pause a little bit before using the word *interactions*. I'm not really sure if that's the right thing to call it. Is relations better? Should I just have called it hooking up or does that just refer to sex?

"No, we were never together. We never dated."

"Where were you last night?" I ask, leaning a little closer to him in an attempt to put on a bit of pressure.

"I was with Natalie," he says nonchalantly as if he doesn't have a care in the world.

"Natalie?" I ask, pretending to be clueless.

"Yeah, Natalie D'Achille."

"Your girlfriend?"

I take out my notepad and write down the name showing it to him to make sure that I have the correct spelling.

"Can you give me her phone number and address?"

"Yeah, I guess," he says, grabbing his phone out of his pocket.

Neil scrolls for her name and then gives me the info.

"You and Natalie, you're together?"

"Yeah. We've been together for years. Well, on and off. You know how it is."

Suddenly, I have an unexplainable urge to smack the smirk right off his face, but I try to contain myself.

Given the cocky confidence that he has at age thirteen, I can't imagine what kind of monster he might become at eighteen, twenty-five, forty, but I don't really want to find out. Besides, who knows? It might just be an act, a form of self-protection and he's actually a nice guy underneath it all.

Someone yells from upstairs and Mrs. Goss excuses herself to attend to his little brother or sister. For a moment, Neil and I are alone.

"Neil," I say, trying to be as pleasant and open as possible. "You can tell me anything. Your mom isn't in here right now and I'm not going to judge. I am just trying to find my sister. It's really important. Did you see her at all last night?"

"No, I already said that I didn't. I was with Natalie. We studied together and then hung out and made out for a bit, but that's it."

"What time was this?"

"I don't know, from like six until ten or so, I think."

I am about to press him some more, but then Mrs. Goss comes back and I realize that I'm not going to get any more out of him. At least, not now.

I DRIVE BACK HOME, wondering if any of this is relevant. I don't seem to be any closer to figuring out what happened to Violet than I was earlier. Neil was a long shot. It's probably Kaylee Dillinger who I have to focus on and her mom, Nancy.

So far, they're sticking to one story.

My mind goes in circles as I try to figure out what could have happened. They dropped her off, but they didn't see her go inside.

Could someone have snatched her before she got there or maybe she left on her own? Maybe she had plans to meet up with someone, a boyfriend, a secret boyfriend that she didn't tell anyone about. Maybe Kaylee knows who this person is and isn't saying. Maybe Kaylee and Nancy never dropped her off there in the first place.

There are so many possibilities and yet I'm at a standstill. I'm no closer to finding her than I was earlier. I know that I need to go talk to the cops again. They might have checked the cameras by now and I still want to do my own search of the neighborhood.

When I get back to my mom's house, I do a perimeter drive around and then get out of the car and actually walk in a grid-like pattern to check for anything that can be found. This is what you do when you search for missing people. You cover a very small area and you look everywhere you can, taking pictures of anything suspicious just in case. Two hours later, I come up empty-handed.

Back inside, I sit down at the kitchen table and tell Mom everything that I've learned.

"So why did you go to this Neil Goss's house? What was the point?"

"I don't know. It was just a whim. She mentioned him. She mentioned that Violet liked him. So, I thought maybe they had made some sort of date or something and met up after they dropped her off, but it was a long shot as I said."

Mom nods. She looks tired now with big black circles under her eyes. I wonder if she slept more than a few hours last night.

"How are you?" I ask.

She shakes her head and says, "You don't want to know." She pulls out a cigarette and this time doesn't go outside.

"You promised me that you were going to quit," I say.

“Yeah, I did,” she says, taking a long drag. “So what?”

“I thought that you usually smoked out there?”

“Yes, but it’s cold now and it’s not like Violet is here to inhale all of that secondhand smoke.”

That statement sends a shudder through me. Does she know something I don’t?

"Don't give up, okay?” I say, squeezing her hand. “It hasn't been that long. She could still just be out with a friend, maybe she fell asleep on his couch or her couch and she’ll just walk through the door any minute now, crying and apologizing profusely."

"You're talking about yourself. That's not Violet.”

Mom’s words cut deep.

I hate the tone of her voice. I hate how certain she is that something is really wrong. I know that Violet has a history of being a good girl, but she's thirteen and that might have changed overnight.

Who knows, right?

I have to hold on to some hope. It's weird being in this position. As a detective, I'm usually the one that's more cynical, pessimistic, maybe even so-called realistic about the possibilities.

It is always the families who hold onto hope until there's nothing left. They grab onto it and they just hold it. It's like water in between their fingers. It flows through and yet they continue to grasp onto it. In this case, I want my mom to do a little bit of that grasping. I want her to have a little bit of hope because I certainly can't have enough for the both of us.

I make myself another cup of coffee and take it out to the living room. I took a day off from work today, but I'm nervous to check my emails and calls because I don't want to be called back.

If they don't find out more details about that dead girl we found hanging from the tree, then I'll have more time here. If they do, then I'll have to go back and then what? What happens to Violet and her case?

I don't sit on the couch for too long. Two cups of coffee and that's it. Then I decide to take a drive out to see Captain Talarico and anyone else working this case.

THE BIG BEAR Sheriff's Station is located right in the center of town and looks like your quintessential small town police department; low ceilings with a wide roof.

There's somebody up front in a uniform, clearing the walkways of the snow. I nod hello and walk through the glass doors.

"I'm here to see Captain Talarico," I say to the person at the front desk.

"I think he's in his office right now. Let me double check."

I expect her to pick up the phone and call but instead, she just leans over her desk and peeks around the corner.

"Yes, there he is. He doesn't look busy. Why don't you go right ahead?"

Captain Talarico sits in his office at a metal desk with a computer to one side eating a messy sandwich. There's relish and onion bits everywhere, on a big piece of spread out paper drenched in oil. He's holding the sandwich with both hands, more like wrestling with it, as he takes big chunks out with his teeth.

"Excuse me, I'm here to see Captain Talarico," I say, knocking on the door. "I'm Kaitlyn Carr, the detective from the LAPD."

It's hard for me to decide whether I should introduce myself as Detective Carr or just Kaitlyn Carr because I don't want anyone thinking that I'm pulling rank or anything like that. It's hard to know how people will respond to you, one way or the other.

"Come in," he says, pointing to one of two chairs in front of his desk.

The desk is covered in papers along with notepads and folders strewn all around. There's a big ficus plant in the corner gathering dust and a bar of fluorescent light right above our heads casts long unflattering shadows across everything.

"I just wanted to pop in and ask you about what's happening with Violet's case. Any news? Any updates?"

He finishes his sandwich by licking each one of his fingers and then wiping them off with the napkin soaked in oil before washing it all down with a few generous gulps of his thirty-ounce soda.

"You've been a bad girl," he says, cockily tilting his head.

"What do you mean?"

"Well, I got a call from Mr. Goss, the prosecutor, and he told me that you showed up at seven o'clock this morning at his house and were bothering his son with questions about somebody he goes to school with."

"I wasn't bothering his son. I just asked him a few questions. So what?" I shrug, adjusting my position in the chair.

"Why did you do that?" he asks, sucking on the soda so intensely that it makes a loud gurgling sound.

"When I talked to Kaylee Dillinger, she mentioned that Violet had a crush on this kid named Neil and he was mean to her and at one point they may have had a thing."

"Well, thanks for putting them on alert," Captain Talarico says, shaking his head with disapproval.

"I didn't mean to do that."

"No, of course you didn't and, of course, you didn't talk to me about any of this prior to getting involved."

I cower in my seat.

“What police department do you work for again, Miss Carr?"

I am very well aware of the fact that he calls me Miss when it’s really Detective and he knows it, but I don’t correct him.

"I know what you're saying," I say, throwing my hands up.

"No, you don't. Answer my damn question,” he says, staring straight into my eyes.

"I work for the LAPD."

"Yes, you do. What department is investigating this possible missing person’s case?"

"Big Bear Sheriff’s Station."

"Exactly. So therefore, you have no jurisdiction here whatsoever and I would appreciate it if you didn't go around, mucking up this case by alerting all of the possible suspects that they may be possible suspects."

I feel like a fool. I had no idea Neil’s dad was a prosecutor. Kaylee just told me that he was an attorney, but I should have found out more before I just showed up there.

"I didn't know that he’s a prosecutor,” I say quietly, admitting my mistake without coming right out with it.

Suddenly, his tone seems to change. His face relaxes a bit. The tension dissipates from his forehead.

"Listen," Captain Talarico says, leaning closer to me across the desk. "I know that you're very worried about your sister and I totally understand that, but you can't be doing this investigation on your own."

I nod.

"Mr. Goss was an attorney, a very prominent defense attorney. That's how he paid for that big mansion on the lake. Then he decided to work for the District Attorney's office. I guess he has his sights set on some sort of judgeship or something in the future. Who knows? Anyway, he's a major pain in the ass. He makes life very difficult for this department. I'm sure that I don't have to tell you this but that's not exactly conducive to solving and prosecuting crimes."

"So… what are you saying exactly?" I ask.

"I'm saying that you have to stay away from Neil Goss."

"I don't even know if he's involved," I say.

"Exactly. Let us do some more digging. Let us talk to some more of their friends before we approach him. He may have nothing to do with this at all and, if that's the case, then it saves me a migraine from dealing with his father."

I nod. I want to admit that I didn't know any of this was going on, but I keep my mouth shut. I already feel like a major fool.

"So, what are you going to do now? What's the plan?"

"We'll be talking to her friends and family members," Captain Talarico says, leaning back in his chair. He opens his mouth to burp but then relaxes when nothing comes out.

"We're going to interview your mom again. We're going to talk to all the kids at school. Anyone that she had any relationship with. Someone has to know something. Who knows? Maybe she'll just come home today and this whole thing will be over. Then you can go back to LA."

"You'd like that," I say with a joke.

He looks at me, tilts his head again, and admits, "Yes, I would like that very much, Detective Carr."

I smile and silently thank him for using the right title.

Before I leave, I share some of what I have found out with the captain. I tell him exactly what Neil told me, as well as Kaylee and Nancy, just in case there are any discrepancies.

When I get back in the car, the sun is high in the sky, beating down, making me sweat in my coat. I pull it off and take the sweater off with it leaving just the t-shirt. I'm not sure where to go now. I want to go talk to Natalie but I know that she's in school and I did promise Captain Talarico that I'd hold off on any further investigation.

On the drive back home, I get a call. It's my boss, Captain Medvil. As soon as I see the name on the screen, my breath gets caught in the back of my throat.

I know that I have to take this call, but I don't want to. He doesn't call me often and this means that something major has happened, but what?

I click accept and hold my breath. He doesn't say hello or ask how I'm doing. There is no chitchat.

"We have identified the girl," he says and my heart drops.

8

"She's thirteen years old," Captain Medvil barks into my ear. "Her name is Courtney Reynard and she lives in Brentwood. We need to interview her parents, ASAP. The deputy is telling them about the news right now."

"Okay," I say after a long pause.

"Okay, what? Are you going to do it or not?"

"Yes. When?" I ask, my mind going blank.

I'm not sure how to deal with this.

How do I get back to do my job and how do I to stay here to find my sister?

"I don't know if you know, Captain Medvil, but I took a day off because my sister didn't come home last night."

“Oh…no…I didn't realize that."

"I'm in Big Bear right now, my mom’s house. Violet was supposed to come home last night and she didn't. She got dropped off and she never came inside, so my mom was really freaking out. We're working with police up here and just trying to find her."

"Okay," he says.

"Any chance she just ran away?"

"No, I highly doubt that. She has always been a really good kid."

"Well, things change when they start to grow up. Their hormones make them go nuts."

I nod trying to be polite and courteous.

Captain Medvil has three kids of his own, one of whom has been arrested for a driving under the influence charge, just a few months ago. He doesn't have the best opinion of teenagers, if I were to put it lightly.

"I'm sorry about your sister, but Courtney Reynard's parents need to be interviewed and you have a special touch with parents, as you know."

He's referring to my old case, the one in which I got the parents to finally admit what their son had done.

I hate to say that was the highlight of my career up to this point, but it sort of was. Without their testimony, we'd have nothing. No DNA, no trace evidence, no witnesses. But after a few long conversations with me, things changed.

"They are the last ones who saw her alive and we need their help to figure out who she is," the captain says.

Of course, he isn't telling me anything I don't already know.

I swallow hard and the lump in the back of my throat seems to grow in size.

My mind is going a mile a minute.

I don't know what to do.

I know that I have to get back for work and these interviews have to be conducted as soon as possible.

But what about Violet?

"The sheriff's department is on top of it, right?" Captain Medvil asks, reading my mind. "Why don't you drive down here, do these interviews, and then go back up?"

"Okay, I guess I can do that." I nod.

"Carr," Captain Medvil says right before I hang up.

"Yes?"

"Everything's going to be okay. Teenage girls run away all the time."

"Yeah, I guess," I mumble, not at all convinced.

"Listen, I know that in our line of work, the worst thing always happens. It's always that terrible eventuality and it gives us a really pessimistic view of the world. But in reality, that is often not the case. Most of the time, it's not a murder. Most of the time, a kid goes missing and nothing bad happens. We just tend to see the negative in the world."

"Uh-huh," I mumble.

"I just want you keep that in mind when you think about your sister. Of course, go through the proper channels and try to find her as soon as possible, but don't let your pessimism bring you down."

I nod and hang up the phone. His words reverberate in my mind and I try to take what he has said to heart.

He's right, of course. In this line of work, you tend to see the worst in everything and then expect to see that in your day-to-day life. But the world doesn't run according to Murphy's Law.

Someone doesn't call you back and you think, maybe something bad has happened. Maybe they got into a car accident. But most of the time, it’s something simple like, their phone just died.

Maybe Violet just slept over at a friend's house and forgot to call. Maybe she didn't want Kaylee or Mom to know that she went out with someone she shouldn’t have. These are both definite possibilities.

“Okay," I say to myself, pulling into Mom’s driveway. “It's going to be okay. I just have to go back to LA, do these interviews, and then get back here as soon as possible.”

I get home and find my mom in the backyard getting something out of the shed. We don't have a garage. We never had one, even though my mom had planned to have one built for years. Without one, the house has basically no storage. A few years ago, Mom finally gave in and bought one of those sheds from Home Depot and had a local kid put it together.

I find her all the way in the back, searching for something through all the piles of boxes and stuff stored in garbage bags. She has been threatening to take most of them to the thrift store, but I doubt that they’ll want it and it will probably end up in the dump.

My mom isn't exactly a clean freak. I wouldn't say that her house is particularly dirty or anything like that, but she tends to hoard and keep things until they stop serving their purpose. Of course, she can't keep everything in the house, so she moves things to the shed until they become so decrepit that she has to throw them away.

Of course, most of the boxes and bags out back are meant for the Salvation Army or one of the other thrift stores, but she always thinks that there will be a use for things that she no longer needs.

I'm the one that likes to give stuff away.

Ever since I was a little kid, having grown up in this house where everything was always kept, including all of the plastic bags and all of the utensils from takeout, I feel overwhelmed by stuff. It actually gives me anxiety just to be surrounded by crap.

I'd rather have nearly nothing than all of this, while she seems to be the complete opposite. I guess that explains a lot about my apartment back in LA.

My furniture is anything but sparse. I guess I would call it a minimalist look to try to make it seem like I'm sophisticated, but in reality, I just don't like owning things.

"What are you doing back here?" I ask, leaning against the doorway. The shed is just barely tall enough for me to stand up straight and I am 5'5".

"Just looking for this box of books that Violet had me put out here a few days ago," Mom says, wiping her brow with the back of her hand. "She was so insistent. She just didn't want to have them in her room anymore."

I eye the concave ceiling and wonder how many snowfalls it will last before totally succumbing to the elements. You have to clear the roof all the time to make sure that it doesn't cave in from all of the snow in the winter, and, of course, that wasn't something we considered when we saw it in July sitting in front of Home Depot in all of its glory.

"You know, none of this would be happening if your dad was still around. We'd have the garage and we would've gotten the right shed," Mom says, exasperated.

That's always her go-to line. If only Dad were still around then everything would be great. As if things were always great when he was around.

I don't say anything even though I really want to. To say something would be cruel.

She has lost her husband and now her daughter is missing. We shouldn't be arguing about who's at fault for this terrible, terrible shed.

"How about this, Mom? How about I get you a new one for your birthday next year?" I offer, looking around at the paper-thin, peeling walls.

She glares at me. Dressed in a suede jacket, weathered waterproof boots, and a pair of faded jeans, Mom stands hunched over so as to not hit her head on the ceiling. Her hair is pulled up to the top of her head and her face actually looks like it has a little bit of color to it after all of this physical exertion.

"Are you serious?" she asks, putting her hand on her hip.

"What do you mean?"

"Are you seriously asking me whether you can get me a shed for my birthday?" She accentuates the words *shed* and *birthday* and gives me so much attitude that I almost laugh.

"Well, it's something you need."

"Birthdays aren't about need. You, of all people, should know that. Birthdays are about indulgences and fun. Honestly, you're just like your father. Do you know that he actually got me a floor for my birthday once?"

“A floor?”

"Yeah. We had this really old linoleum tile floor in the kitchen, right around the time that you were born, and so for my birthday, he decided that he would replace it and lay it all down himself. It's not that I didn't appreciate the effort, but you know what? He walks on the floor as well. He enjoys the floor. Why the hell does it have to be *my* birthday present?"

I laugh and she laughs as well. For a moment there, we forget about everything that has gone wrong in our family and just enjoy each other's company.

"I have to go back to LA," I say, walking over to the bin with my old toys.

I run my fingers along the ear of one of my stuffed rabbits. Ralph is cold to the touch with worn fur and tired glass eyes, but still very much loved. His ears are round rather than elongated and he has an inexplicably large, orange tail. Actually, it's quite generous of me to call Ralph a rabbit since looking at him now he looks more like a rabbit/fox hybrid or maybe even an animal unknown to science. But I've always thought of him as a rabbit and that's what he will always be.

"I can't believe that you kept Ralph," I say, pulling him into a tight hug. I cradle him in my arms like a baby, overwhelmed by all of the love that comes pouring out of him.

"I keep a lot of things. You never know when someone might want something back."

Mom nods at Ralph and gives me a wink. I force myself to drop him to my side, pretending that I'm not overjoyed by the fact that she had kept him.

"What are you looking for in that box of books?" I ask, changing the subject.

"I don't know," she says with a shrug. "They're all of your old *Sweet Valley High* books. You remember them?"

I smile at the corner of my lips. How could I forget? I whizzed through them at age eleven or twelve. I read three books a day until I'd read them all and then read them again and again. There was no such thing as binging Netflix back then, but I was definitely on a binge.

"Did Violet like them?" I ask.

"She loved them. I didn't really think they were her style, since she prefers fantasy, but I think she enjoyed them because she knew that they were *your* favorite."

I nod. It's weird to think back to the little girl that I used to be; the little, bright, friendly girl who loved *Sweet Valley High* and *the Babysitter's Club* books and dressed exclusively in pink and fuchsia.

The whole right side of the shed contains boxes of my stuff, my old books, my old clothes, my old toys, going back to toddlerhood. Some of these things Mom reused and gave to Violet to play with, but most of them, she just kept for the sake of it. It's weird to see your whole life presented like this; one box piled on top of the other, each one holding bundles of memories.

"You sure did like pink," Mom says with a smirk, looking me up and down and undoubtably examining my black wardrobe with a scorn.

Mom always thought I'd be a teacher or maybe a librarian like her since I loved to read so much, but a detective? Never.

She did not have much to say when I told her that I was going to go to the police academy after college. I just sort of came home and announced it to her one Thanksgiving, as if it was something that I had been thinking about for a long time.

My mom and I have always had a complicated relationship. Our personalities are rather mismatched.

Her nervous energy has always put me on edge. I grew up entrenched in a perpetual state of panic. But I didn't want to be seen as someone who worried a lot, so I hid that part of me.

When it came to big decisions, I had to make them on my own. I couldn't bring myself to tell my mom what I was thinking while I was thinking it. I had to reach a decision and then tell her what I'd decided to do.

On TV, parents are often portrayed as sounding boards, someone who gives advice and someone you can come to for those things, but that wasn't what I ever had with my mom, or my dad, for that matter. They were people who always got only the final decisions.

Violet was only four when I came home and announced that I had enrolled and would be starting my training in a few weeks. Mom asked me all about the logistics, the *when* and *how*, but she never really asked *why*.

I mean, she did in a way, but she never got down to the truth. I remember telling her that the pay would be good and with overtime, I could make decent money. I was single. I wasn't planning on having kids anytime soon, so why not? Who knew, I might even become a detective one day.

It finally happened, many years later, and yet we still haven't talked about the *why*.

"Okay, here it is," Mom says, picking up an old bathrobe and a few old costumes from Halloween from years ago. There are more *Sweet Valley High* books underneath.

"How did they end up all the way in here?" I ask. "Didn't you just say that she just had them in her room?"

"Yeah, but she wanted to clear out some stuff and donate. You know how she was. You know how she *is*," Mom corrects herself, but we both hang on that word *was* for a while.

Up until this point, I haven't allowed myself to think of Violet in the past tense.

"Mom, are you trying to tell me something?"

"No. Of course not."

"Do you know where Violet is?"

"What are you talking about?" she snaps.

I shake my head and say, "Just that you used *was*."

"Well, I misspoke."

I nod even though I don't believe her. My mom has been a librarian for many years and she rarely misspeaks.

I decide not to press her on it, for now.

Instead, I focus on the box. Something about the box doesn't make sense. First of all, it's all the way in the back of the shed. The Halloween costumes are old from years ago, along with the bathrobe that I haven't seen since at least 2012. If Violet had put the books into the shed, she would have stuck them into some other box out front in order to get in and out of this place as soon as she could.

Why put them all the way in the back?

She wasn't someone who liked being in crowded spaces any more than I did, even if it was crammed with all of our old things.

"Violet said that she read through them and she was done," Mom says, reading my mind.

"Why do you need them now?" I ask.

"I was just wondering where it was. She packed up this box and I don't know, I'm at a loss."

I follow Mom back out to the house over the wet, soggy ground, the mud clinging to my boots. I take them off right inside the doorway and Mom plops the box on the kitchen table and takes out all of the contents. On the bottom, she finds a smaller box, the size of a jewelry box, with a few bracelets, two rings, and a necklace. All costume jewelry with no precious stones or metals.

"What is this?" I ask.

"I'm not sure," Mom says, shaking her head. "She usually keeps all of her jewelry in that wooden chest that you gave her last Christmas."

I bought that handmade chest from Etsy, knowing that Violet would love it. It had a beautiful design of an elephant on the front, along with all sorts of carvings that you see in Eastern-religion-inspired designs. I look for the chest in her room, but it's not there.

"Did you move it somewhere?" I yell, looking under her bed. "Where do you think it is?"

"I don't know," Mom says, walking through the door.

"Well, it's not here. How can that be?"

Mom walks over to the desk that Violet uses as her nightstand as well. This is where she sits to do her homework.

There's a little red lamp in the corner that she uses to read *Twilight* and *Harry Potter* and an assortment of other titles.

I look around the room. The bed is a mattress sitting on top of storage containers with drawers where she keeps additional blankets and summer clothes, whatever doesn't fit into her closet.

The closet across from the bed is small with one of those sliding mirror doors that makes you look like you're double the size that you are.

Violet hates that thing as much as I did when this was my room so there's a slender stand-up mirror next to the window to compensate. Another one of my Christmas presents.

Unlike Mom, who gets Violet's clothes from Talbots and other age-inappropriate stores, I have always prided myself in getting her exactly what she wants.

I open the closet door and look through her shoes and clothing. Mom told me that she was wearing jeans and her forest green puffy jacket when she left, along with a beanie.

"What about her combat boots? You know, the Doc Martens?"

"You mean those awful, black, ugly boots that you got her for her eleventh birthday? God, I have no idea where they are," Mom says, rolling her eyes.

"Okay, but they're not here."

"Ugh, good riddance," Mom mutters.

I walk over to rummage through the storage under her bed before checking underneath the bookshelves where she keeps additional shoes and a few more boxes of things.

"Mom, they're not here."

"So what?"

"Well, the chest is missing and so are the combat boots. Was she wearing them when she left?"

"No. I don't think so."

"How can you be sure?"

Mom tilts her head to the side and looks up, thinking, and then finally says, "No, she wasn't wearing them that night. I know because they're awful and I always remember when she has them on."

"What was she wearing?"

"I don't know. Her Uggs, I think."

"Okay, that's something. So, what happened to the Doc Martens? Do you think that she put them in storage?"

"No, absolutely not," Mom says categorically.

There's an exasperation to her voice, like she's resigned to something terrible. "Where are you going with all of this? What's with all these questions?"

"I just don't understand all of these strange inconsistencies," I say.

"What inconsistencies?"

I'd pace back and forth, but it takes me barely a step and a half to get from one side of the room to the other. It's not exactly a bedroom, but it's not exactly a broom closet either. It's something in between.

I walk over to the small window and look at the tree outside covered in snow. The branches lay heavy under all of that white snow. There's a small bird prancing along on one of the dry spots and then she picks up her wings and takes off.

"If Violet wasn't wearing the boots and you know that they are one of her favorites, then *where* are they? Also, where's the chest with her jewelry? Why did she put some of the jewelry with the books into the shed?"

I'm speaking out loud now, sort of asking my mom the questions, but really just trying to process everything that I have just discovered.

It's normal procedure to go through the room and try to find clues as to where the person might have gone, or would have gone, if those clues can be found in the room. But Mom hadn't figured out any of these things when the cops asked her about it and frankly, she hadn't noticed these things either, until I did.

"Why don't you look around here and see what else might be missing?" I say, heading to the kitchen.

I fill up my water bottle and make myself a sandwich from the bread in the pantry and some peanut butter.

"Where are you going?" Mom asks, following me out.

"I have to get back to LA. I have to conduct a few interviews with the parents of a murder victim."

"You do? Now?"

"Either that or someone else is going to get the case. It's just... I need to do this, Mom. I'm the one that was there when they found the girl and I hope that I can close this case quickly."

"What about Violet?"

"I'll try to come back tonight. I'm going to do the interviews and come back either tonight or tomorrow morning, but in the meantime, you need to look around and catalog what's missing. I don't live with her. I don't really know what she uses all the time, but you do. Can you do this for me?"

"What about the chest and the boots? What do they mean?"

"They might mean that she meant to take off, Mom. They might mean that she wanted to go somewhere and she took things that she loved with her."

Mom shakes her head and denies it, "No. No, no. Absolutely not."

"Okay, I know that you don't want to believe this and neither do I, but I really hope that if she is gone, she's gone of her own volition. Don't you?"

Mom shakes her head.

She doesn't want to believe anything at this point. I look at the time.

If I want to get all the way back home and get these interviews done tonight, I have to leave now. Like, as soon as possible.

I grab my bag, which I haven't really unpacked, and throw the sandwich into my purse. I give my mom a brief peck on the cheek and walk out the door.

When I get down the hill, without encountering too much traffic, I let out a sigh of relief. Driving up and down the mountain is kind of a crapshoot. You can do it very quickly and without any incidents, but if there’s an accident, it can take hours. Luckily, everything aligns in my favor and I get to the precinct by four in the afternoon, right when the Reynard family arrives.

When I walk through the front door of the precinct, I notice the distinct smell of Lysol and bleach. Usually, the cleaning people come in the evenings, but everything smells like some sickening conversation of pine, lime, and lemons. I wave hello to some of the other deputies, but I don't have time to chat.

I know that I'm not dressed completely appropriate so I head into the locker room and pull out the suit that I keep there for this exact occasion. It's something that Captain Medvil had mentioned was a good idea and, at first, I remember scoffing at him.

I mean, why would I need to have a suit on hand? I can just go home and change, right?

Well, not always.

I get out of the clothes that I had slept in last night. I wish that I could take a shower, but I don't have time. Instead, I refresh myself with a wet wipe and apply some more makeup.

It's important to look professional and well put-together, especially when you interview family members of victims of crimes. I'm a homicide detective and I can't very well show up in a ratty sweatshirt and ripped jeans.

I take a few moments to collect my thoughts while in the bathroom stall.

On the whole drive down here, I kept trying to make sense of what I'd found out. I realize I don't know if Kaylee or her mom, Nancy, have anything to do with Violet's disappearance.

I kind of doubt that Neil does, either.

But what about *my* mom?

Is she telling me everything?

Is she hiding the fact that they had a big fight and that's why Violet left? I mean, Violet's a teenage girl and it's not like I haven't seen plenty of that in my line of work.

On one hand, finding the fact that her favorite pair of Doc Martens and a box of her jewelry is missing along with her has given me a glimmer of hope.

It could mean that she didn't get kidnapped by a stranger or at least the likelihood of her getting kidnapped by a stranger is a lot less. Perhaps this could even mean that she just took off.

I flush the toilet and walk out of the stall to wash my hands.

Then it hits me. It's not an either/or situation. Both things could be true at the same time.

Cold sweat runs down my armpit and makes a stain on my pressed blouse. Luckily, I'm wearing a matching suit jacket to go with my skirt, so it's not obvious.

Of course, one thing does not mean that the other one didn't happen. Just because Violet took off by herself doesn't mean that she didn't *also* get taken.

9

I leave the locker room with my head held high. The suit, the heels, and the bag that I carry are my armor.

My makeup is flawless. My lips are shining red.

On the outside, I look put together and in control.

That's the point.

On the inside, my stomach is in knots.

I check the moisture on my palms. It's not just a saying, you can't let them see you sweat.

I grab a tissue from my purse and wipe them because I'm going to shake hands and I need Courtney Reynard's parents to know that they are in good hands.

This is all a show, a little dance that I put on and that detectives have put on for years and years.

The people we meet have to see us as solid, unmoving mountains so that that they can let their emotions collide with ours.

It's typically procedure for the homicide detective to notify the next of kin about the deaths, but I was three hours away and Captain Medvil sent someone else in my place.

The victim's parents are now waiting in the back, in one of the nicer interview rooms with plush velvet chairs and clip-art wall decor. This is typically where we meet with the friends and family.

I turn the corner at the water fountain. My heels make a loud clicking sound with each step and I'm keenly aware of how tight my skirt is. It's digging into my waist, making it difficult to breathe, but it sure does make my butt look good.

The fluorescent lights above my head flicker for a moment just as I turn the corner. That's when I run into him, straight on, just like in the fucking movies.

My purse and all of its contents go everywhere just as his folder does.

It takes me a moment to look up at the person I've run into before I reach for my purse and I recognize him immediately.

Perfect. I say silently to myself; I'm definitely not apologizing to him.

"How are you?" Thomas asks.

His hair looks freshly cut in that familiar, short style, popular with police officers. His chest looks puffy and inflated, not so much from exercise, but from an oversized opinion of himself.

He leans over and hands me my purse. A few more things fall out, a lipstick and mascara along with my phone.

"Hey," I say and bite my tongue just as I am about to say, *Come on now. Say you're sorry, Thomas.*

He doesn't. Instead, he just stares deep into my eyes like he used to when we were first together.

"How are you doing?" he asks, after collecting all of the papers from his manila folder.

"I'm good. How are you?" I toss the floss, the powder, and the little foldable comb all back into my purse into no compartment in particular. I want this interaction to be done with as soon as possible.

"Hey, listen, I'm sorry about that," he says, grabbing my hand. Just as I put the purse over my shoulder, I pull away from him and our eyes meet again. "Sorry for bumping into you."

"Yes, me, too," I add with a nod, satisfied but not fully. "Listen, I have to go."

"Yeah, me, too. Of course," he says, hesitating.

He turns slowly on his heel and continues to stare at the back of my head all the way down the hallway. I can feel his gaze. It sends shivers up my spine. It makes me want to turn around, but I tell myself to stay strong.

No, do not give him the satisfaction. I don't.

It would be a lie to say that running into Thomas Abrams, my ex-boyfriend, doesn't throw me a little bit off course as I walk over to speak with the Reynards. They sit huddled together like two doves, leaning on each other for support, waiting for me to bring them some answers. The problem is that I don't have any. I take a deep breath and then another and another.

There are a few uniformed officers standing around the water cooler, not too far away from me and I break through their huddle to get some water. Of course, I've heard that it's not a good idea to date people you work with, but I didn't realize that it would be this difficult. Every time I interact with him, or even just see him out of the corner of my eye, I regret the fact that I didn't press charges that night.

What would this be like if I had?

How many of these cops would take his side and how many would take mine?

Thomas is popular. Thomas has many friends. He's the kind of guy that everyone likes.

He can bullshit about just about anything; sports, girls, chicken wings. He's inoffensive in that way that fresh pizza from a chain restaurant is inoffensive. Always good, but not particularly exciting to the pallet.

It's something that you can depend on, of course, unless you're his girlfriend, then he's not particularly dependable or safe. In fact, he might even give you food poisoning.

I finish one cup of water and toss the little cone into the trash. Then, I head straight inside.

Swinging the door open, I introduce myself to the Reynards.

When I come into the room, they break out of their huddle and look up at me at the same time. Mr. Reynard puts his arm on his wife's back, as if to prop her up for the news to come.

They already know what happened. Well, a little bit about it, anyway. They had been notified that their daughter's body had been found hanging from a tree in Runyon Canyon and they have identified her with the medical examiner.

This is the thing that I always hate about my job. Though the pursuit of the bad guy and getting justice for the victim and the victim's families always feels good, this part, this wallowing in other people's sorrow, does not.

I wish I could be like some of the other people here who could just turn off their feelings, shut them down, or perhaps just bury them at the bottom of a bottle. I'm not like that. I let their emotions wash over me and I can't help but feel some of it deep in my soul.

I introduce myself and shake their hands.

Mr. Reynard looks like the kind of guy who would give you a strong handshake on any other occasion except for this one. Mrs. Reynard doesn't even try. Her hand is limp and barely there. I hold her hand in my palm for only a few moments before she pulls away.

"How could this happen?" she asks, shaking her head, tears welling up in her eyes.

“That's what we're here to find out,” I assure her, but my words are a lot less than adequate. "I have to go over a few things with you, Mr. and Mrs. Reynard. Would you mind telling me exactly when the last time was that you saw Courtney?"

"She went to bed," Mr. Reynard says, shaking his head. "She went to bed and then she was gone."

"What time was that?"

"I don't know. Nine or so."

"Does she usually go to bed that early?" I ask, knowing full well that that's not a particularly common thing for teenagers to do.

"Well, she said she was going to bed. She said goodnight and kissed everyone on the cheek." When he says that, his wife breaks down in tears.

"I have to tell her everything," Mr. Reynard says.

"Please continue," I urge him.

He pauses for a moment, not knowing how to continue.

"You said that she kissed everyone. Who is everyone, exactly?"

"We were downstairs, hanging out in the kitchen, having a glass of wine. Maureen had just put down our five-year-old. Well, she was going to, he was not exactly cooperating. So, he was staying up a little late, nine o'clock."

I nod and make a note of that in my notebook.

"Okay, please go on."

"Well, I don't know," Mr. Reynard says, propping his head up with one hand as he crosses his arms.

He has thick, lustrous hair that was once a beautiful color of chestnut. Now there are only a few strands of that color left. The rest has been replaced by a coarse, silver color that makes him a little bit uneasy as he touches it.

"I'm not sure what you want me to say," Mr. Reynard says, exasperated. "I don't know what any of this has to do with what happened. She's not there. I don't know what time she left."

"Okay, please, let's stay calm," I say, being careful to use the words "let's stay calm" rather than "calm down." It puts the job of being calm on all of us in the room, rather than creating an accusation of him being the only one who is getting upset. This seems to work.

I wait for him to collect his thoughts, but then Mrs. Reynard steps up.

"The last time that we saw her was around nine o'clock. She went upstairs to bed. She went around and kissed all of us and said that she was tired. She was going to study a little bit and that's it."

"Okay, good," I say, nodding. "By all of us, you mean you two and your son?"

"Yes, our five-year-old, Dennis. He was still up, unfortunately, or, I don't know. Maybe not."

I nod. I wonder if he knows and, if not, for how long he'll be able to live in a world in which his sister is still alive.

"That was the last time you heard from her?" I ask.

"No," Mrs. Reynard says, looking down at her pink lacquered nails. The harsh fluorescent light above makes them look a lot less elegant than they are. "I didn't see her again after that. She didn't come down for breakfast, and that's when we knew something was wrong. She's a good girl, she studies hard. I have no idea how she could have left or why or why someone would have taken her."

That's not likely, I want to tell them, but this isn't the right time. The thing is that there is no evidence of...

"What, what is it?" Mrs. Reynard asks. "You don't think anyone took her?" It feels almost like she can read my mind.

"Um," I hesitate.

I know that I shouldn't come right out with this, but I already get the feeling that these people had nothing to do with their daughter's disappearance.

I know that detectives put way too much stress on their feelings and their so-called intuition, but the thing is that most of the time, that's all we have going for us.

Yes, there's DNA, fingerprints, and all of that jazz, but the thing that leads us in one particular direction over another at the very beginning of an investigation is that *hunch*, the feeling of something being off.

We study people.

We study how they react to things.

We analyze them.

That's why sometimes innocent people get imprisoned.

They don't have the right reactions. They don't say the right things. They don't fit into a nice little box. But in this case, all I see are two parents broken by their daughter's disappearance.

"We've had officers go through your home and there is no evidence of any sort of breaking and entering," I say.

"What does that mean?" Mr. Reynard barks at me.

"It means that in all likelihood, Courtney took off of her own volition. She left because she wanted to."

They nod just a little bit, trying to process what I'm saying.

"No, no, no. Why would she do that?" Mrs. Reynard says, shaking her head.

Her hair has recently been blown out and I wonder if it has been done by a professional. Her makeup is flawless, even though she has been crying. Just a little bit is smeared around the eyes, but otherwise holding up just perfectly.

"No. She wouldn't have left. She didn't have anywhere to go. Of course, she doesn't drive yet," she adds.

"I know. That's what I actually wanted to talk to you about. Is there any chance that she had a friend pick her up, an *older* friend?"

"Three years older?" Mr. Reynard pipes in. "Is that the kind of girl that you think that she is?"

This takes me by surprise. Now it's my turn to shake my head and furrow my brow.

"I'm not sure what you mean by that."

"Well, what are you saying exactly? Are you saying that our daughter was hanging out with sixteen year olds and just decided to sneak out and go where exactly? Why would she be found in Runyon Canyon Park? She has never been in that part of town."

"I don't have any answers to any of these questions, Mr. Reynard," I say. "That's actually what I want to ask *you* about."

This turnaround in the conversation catches me off guard. I don't know why this triggered him so much, why he got so angry at my suggesting that his daughter would hang out with someone with a license. It's not completely unheard of.

I excuse myself for a moment.

Out in the hallway, I go around the corner and into another room. This is the place where all of my colleagues are gathered watching the interview. Captain Medvil gives me an approving look.

"What do you think?" I ask, walking up to him.

They've all been gathered around two monitors, which are sending out the feed from the interview room. There are closeups on both of their faces along with mine.

"I don't know. I thought that they were just a normal couple, but he did get a little bit upset about you suggesting that she snuck out," Captain Medvil says.

"I know. I don't know what to make of that. I mean, is he just your average controlling father or is there more to it?"

"Why don't you go and press him a little bit more?" he suggests, leaning back against the wall and thinking. No one else has any other suggestions. Forensic evidence is still being processed, but so far no fingerprints have been found.

I come back into the room with a renewed sense of purpose. I bring in two coffees, one for each of them, along with a few packs of M&M's and some candy. Mrs. Reynard says no a little bit too quickly, but keeps eyeing the candy like it's something that she wants but can't have.

"Can you tell me a little bit about yourselves?" I ask, popping a yellow peanut M&M in my mouth and biting through the thin candy shell to the delicious chocolate inside.

"Like what? What do you want to know?"

"Just what it is you do for a living, sir?"

"I'm an oral surgeon."

I nod, having only a general idea of what that is.

"I do teeth when there are emergencies. Like when there's an accident, somebody gets hit by a car, their mouth gets injured, they need a whole bunch of reconstruction done. That's the kind of thing I do."

"You work where?"

"Cedars-Sinai. Everywhere, actually. Sometimes I fly out to San Francisco, depending on where they need me."

"Okay. And you, Mrs. Reynard?"

"Well, I used to be a dental hygienist, but not anymore. I haven't worked since Courtney was little. I do a lot of volunteering and fundraising."

"And what were you doing during the day, up until that point?"

"I don't know." She shakes her head. "I went shopping for a bit, had lunch with a few girlfriends, came back, started dinner, your usual things."

"What about your son, Dennis?" I look at my notes to remember his name.

"Did you pick him up from school?"

"No, I have a nanny to do that."

"Okay." I nod.

"Of course," I want to say quietly to myself, but I'm not here to judge or to make those kind of assumptions.

I ask Mr. Reynard for the same information and he also says that he got back just in time for dinner. The four of them had dinner together around six, hung out in the living room, watched some television, and then Courtney decided to go upstairs to finish her homework and then go to bed.

"So, let me tell you what we know," I say, looking through the notes in my notebook. "The officers who analyzed the scene found that her window to her room on the second floor was closed and locked from the inside."

"Okay." Mr. Reynard nods.

"What does that mean?" Mrs. Reynard asks.

"Well, it means that if she snuck out on her own, then she did not do it through the window. She just came right downstairs and walked out. It also means that no one took her from her room directly."

"They couldn't have come in through the front door." Ms. Reynard looks at her husband. "We have the alarm set up."

"So that's what I was going to ask you. Did you have the alarm set up that night?"

"Yes, we do. Every night. My husband is paranoid about that kind of thing."

"What about cameras? Do you have some sort of doorbell camera or anything like that?"

"Yes, we do." Mr. Reynard nods. "I have it on my phone."

He pulls out his phone and checks the date. He goes back to the night of the incident and clicks through the images.

"How long do these stay here?"

"For a week and then they get saved onto iCloud where I can then delete manually."

"Okay, well, we're going to have to have our team look at them."

"Yes, of course," Mr. Reynard says, but he shows me briefly what happened that night.

Nothing of consequence.

The camera comes on when it detects motion on the front porch and there was none of that after six o'clock in the evening.

"What does this mean?" Mrs. Reynard says when I sit back in the chair and process everything that has happened, or rather not happened.

"Well, it means that we know that she left the house, correct?"

"Of course." Mrs. Reynard nods.

"Well, she didn't go out the front door and she didn't climb out of her window, because it was locked from the inside."

"Okay."

"Is there any other way that she could have left the house?"

"Maybe the garage."

"Okay, the garage."

"Or the back door or the sliding door through the kitchen," Mrs. Reynard suggests.

"You don't have any cameras pointed there?"

"No. No, we don't."

I nod and admit, "Yeah. Those are all options. So, do you have some sort of sound that comes on inside the house when a door opens?"

Mrs.. Reynard looks from side to side, trying to remember.

"Yes, we do," she says, pointing her finger in my face. "When you open the laundry room going to the garage, it makes a sound like a little ding. The same thing happens when you open the door that goes out of the garage, out to where the cans are."

"What about the sliding door and the kitchen?"

"No." She shakes her head categorically. "No, that one doesn't make a sound."

"Okay. So, no sound there and no camera there. Courtney would know this as well, right?"

"Yes, but I don't know how this makes any sense," Mr. Reynard says, his words tumbling over one another.

"What do you mean, sir?" I ask.

"Well, why does it even matter which door she went through or what happened? I don't understand the whole point of this conversation. What was she even doing in Runyon Canyon? How did she get there?"

"That's what I'm trying to figure out, sir. That's why I need all of these answers. Now we know that she left using that sliding door and she would be the one that knew... So, unless someone took her who knew exactly which door wouldn't have the camera on it and wouldn't make a sound, she's the one who left voluntarily through it."

He nods, but still looks a little bit upset and lost. Suddenly my opinion of him shifts a little.

Of course, he still appears to be the concerned father that he was initially, but all of this drama that he created as a result of the door and recording conversation gives me a funny feeling that's difficult to describe.

"What about her phone? Did she ever leave her phone to go anywhere or was she just like the rest of us, keeping it attached to the hip?"

"What do you mean?" Mrs. Reynard asks.

"You know, how we're all addicted to phones. I know I never go anywhere without mine. What about Courtney?"

"No, she was the same way," she says, hanging her head. "She even took it to the bathroom."

"That's what I thought." I nod my head. "Well, we're going to have our forensics people go through her phone and her laptop and all of her social media stuff to see if they find anything of use."

"I just don't understand." Mrs. Reynard shakes her head. "Why would she not have her phone? Why would she leave voluntarily, if what you're saying is right, and leave her phone? I mean, wouldn't she need it? She took it absolutely everywhere."

"I don't have the answer to that question either, but I hope that someday we will."

10

After the preliminary interview is over, I walk back to the room with the screens.

"What do we think?" I ask Captain Medvil and the others.

They look at me and give me a blank stare, a couple of shrugs here and there.

I go through the crime scene in my mind. She was found at one a.m. The medical examiner in the preliminary report, which I had received earlier suggests a time of death all around eleven p.m.

She was found in the middle of the night and it's unclear as to why she left, or with whom, or for what reason. The last time her parents saw her was at nine p.m. She might've left immediately, or she could have waited and someone might have picked her up.

I have one more question. I walk out the door and head toward the interview room. The Reynards are just leaving.

"One more thing," I say and they both lower their heads cowering a little bit. I guess they thought this part was over. "If Courtney did leave through the sliding glass door in your kitchen, would you be able to know that if you were still downstairs?"

They shrug and look at each other. I realize that I'm not getting through.

"What time did you leave the kitchen or go upstairs or do whatever it is that you were going to do?"

Mrs. Reynard looks at her phone and her watch for some reason as if it would provide her with the answer.

"I think we stayed in the kitchen until, what, nine thirty, ten or so, and then we went to the living room to watch some Netflix."

"Okay," I say, shaking my head and tapping my foot on the floor. "From the living room, would you be able to see the sliding door in the kitchen?"

"I don't know. No, I don't think so," Mrs. Reynard says.

I narrow my eyes and I want her to really think about it. She looks at her husband.

He looks perplexed, but not confused.

"No, we wouldn't be able to see her. We were in the living room and that is clear across the dining room on the other side of the house," Mr. Reynard says decisively. "My wife is right. We stayed in the kitchen for a while and so she must not have left then and then we went to the living room around nine forty-five. I'm not sure."

"Okay. Thank you for your time. I'll be in touch."

I walk back down the empty, brightly lit hallway with my hands folded across my chest.

I need a few moments before going inside, a few moments of peace and quiet. I walk past the room with the captain and everyone else on the case and just keep going.

“So, she must have snuck out right around ten at the earliest, but why wouldn't she take her phone? I mean, it's clear why she wouldn't take her laptop, but why not her phone? If someone took her, I don't know. That seems like a far stretch," I mumble to myself, practically speaking out loud just to make sure the thoughts become more concrete in my mind.

No, the most reasonable thing that could have happened is she snuck out, maybe to meet someone or go somewhere and then something happened.

Someone took her.

Unwittingly, my thoughts drift back to Violet.

Why does this girl have to be the same age as her?

Why do these two cases have to be so similar?

No, Violet is not a case, I say to myself, stopping midstep and forcing one foot right next to the other.

I hate wearing heels. They dig into my feet and bind them in the most unnatural way.

I'm not sure what to do. This whole time I've been doing my best not to think about Violet, but it's hard to put her out of my mind completely.

The more time that passes, the more I know that she's probably not gone of her own volition.

It has been almost twenty-four hours since anyone has seen her. The thing is that we can't even put out an Amber Alert or anything like that because we have no idea what car she's possibly traveling in or if she's in one at all.

I'm anxious to get back to Big Bear and to search for her, but I have a job to do here as well.

Whoever did this to this little girl cannot get away.

I take a deep breath before speaking with Captain Medvil. Plastering a casual smile on my face and the *I don't really give a damn* look, I try to appear like every other cop there.

We discuss the Reynards a little bit and a few deputies mention the fact that their house is 7,000 square feet in Brentwood. It's estimated to be about fifteen million on Zillow, meaning it's not your typical rich person's house.

"I had no idea that oral surgeons made that much money," one of deputies says.

"Why, would you have gone to medical school if you knew that they did?" Someone laughs.

"Yeah. I can just imagine you working on people's teeth. You'd throw up right into their mouth," another guy jokes.

"Oh, come on now. Don't be like that, that happened just once."

The other guys continue to mock him and I laugh along with everyone. Captain Medvil is the only one who doesn't.

As I make my way back to my office, I know that there's still so much more information to come in on the Courtney Reynard case: the official medical examiner report, DNA evidence, and fingerprints.

There are just too many unknowns.

With so much time passing and so few clues, I also know a few things that are true for any homicide detective. The first forty-eight hours are imperative.

The vast majority of murderers and suspects in general are arrested within that time period.

After that, the chances of finding out who did it decrease tremendously.

It's hard to know all of these facts because they are things that you almost wish you didn't know.

I wonder sometimes what it's like to go through life without all of these negative statistics in your head.

How many murders go unsolved every year in Los Angeles?

How many people are killed every year in the United States?

How many women are raped?

How many children are molested?

How many parents never come home?

I try not to dwell on it, this is my line of work after all, but it's hard to put all of that aside when your sister is missing.

No matter how hard I try, I can’t help but wonder, is she going to become one of these statistics?

11

"Hey, what are you doing here?" a familiar voice asks somewhere in front of me. I look up from my phone.

It's the guy from the other night, Luke, what though?

I can't remember his last name. He walks over to me and gives me a confident hug.

"It's nice to see you," I say, pulling away.

"Yeah, you, too. Look at you all dressed up."

"Kind of a work thing," I mumble, looking down at my gray pencil skirt.

Luke asks me if I want to grab a cup of coffee.

Of course I do, but I hesitate. I have a lot of paperwork to get through and I have a lot of thoughts to push away about Violet and calls to make about her whereabouts.

But looking into his eyes and the way that he tilts his head while his hair falls into his face, I can't say no.

"Okay, ten minutes, twenty tops. Then I have to get back."

"Of course," Luke says with a casual shrug. "I've got work to do as well."

I like the swagger and the confidence in his voice. It's so easy and casual without much pretense.

We walk downstairs to the coffee bar on the corner. This is a place where all the cops go unless you want to drink the stale lukewarm crap they have inside.

We get in line behind a few uniformed officers. Luke stands so close to me that I can feel his breath on the back of my head, and I like it.

"So, what are you doing here?" I ask, realizing that I don't even know where he works. "Are you stalking me?"

"Ha." He laughs. "You wish."

The line is quite long with at least five people ahead of us.

I don't mind. It gives us more time to chat and get to know each other. I've texted him a little bit, small details here and there about my sister, but this is the first time that we have really talked since that night that we were together.

"What's going on with Violet?"

I don't know if he's pivoting the conversation to something else or avoiding talking about himself, but I take the bait.

"Nothing new. I talked to a few of Violet's friends, this guy she liked. I don't know. They seemed kind of suspicious, but who the heck knows with teenagers?"

"Yeah, they're not like regular perpetrators, huh?" He laughs. "I don't have much experience interviewing thirteen year olds, thank God, but I get the sense that teenagers in general are kind of like sociopaths. Egomaniacal, self-centered, impossible to break."

"What's his dad do?" Luke asks.

"He's a prosecutor."

"Nope. Nada."

"What are you talking about?"

"Well, first of all, his father is an attorney. Kids whose fathers are lawyers all... Okay, let me put it this way. All kids are full of crap, but kids whose fathers are attorneys are so full of crap, they need plumbers."

"I don't think so," I say, shaking my head.

"How many kids do you know?"

"I don't know, a few. My sister," I admit.

Though I guess she is really the only one.

"Well, I have four brothers."

"Four brothers?" I gasp.

"Yep. I'm the youngest. Lucky number five. My parents stopped trying for a girl after that. They figured boys is all they're going to get."

"Wow." I laugh. "Surprised they didn't stop earlier."

"My point is I grew up with a lot of teenagers," he says, shaking his head. "They were older than me, but I saw how they operated. They lied. They cheated. They did anything they could to get away with whatever they wanted."

"Maybe you're right. I don't know. I was the oldest and I sort of snuck out a little bit here and there. Got into a lot of fights with my mom. This kid, Neil, he was different. He was so confident. So cocky. It's like the world owes him something. You know?"

"I know exactly the type. Usually, the more popular they are at the younger age, the worse their attitude is. Especially if no one at home puts them in their place."

"You should've seen this guy's house. It's a mansion."

"You've been to places like that around here, right?" he asks. "I mean, we are talking about LA."

"But people here work in the movies. Big Bear is a small town, mainly a tourist destination, a lot of second homes, that kind of thing. I grew up there. I don't remember anyone I knew at that school who had a house like that. That's bound to go to your head."

I look at his shoulders. Sometimes with certain people, you can tell that that's where they carry their tension. It's like the whole world focuses itself right there below the neck in between the shoulder blades and nothing is ever going to change that.

With Luke, it seems a little bit different.

There's a casualness to him that's difficult to describe.

It's like nothing bothers him, but in a good way.

He's not egocentric or arrogant.

Just still.

At peace.

Someone who knows who he is.

"Do you surf?" I ask.

He tilts his head to one side. I now know that's a move of his. A little bit to the side and a little bit forward to get my attention.

"How do you know?" he asks.

I shrug and shake my head a little bit. Our eyes meet and he doesn't look away.

I want to, but I can't.

The line moves up.

One more person walks away with a cup.

Our time is running out.

"Do you?"

"Do I what?" I ask.

"Do you surf?"

"No. I've never been."

"You live in LA and you've never been surfing?"

"No." I laugh, shaking my head.

"Seriously?"

"Seriously, of course. Why would I lie to you about that?"

"Just seems kind of odd," he says. "Well, that settles it. I guess I'll have to take you. You free tomorrow morning?"

"Oh, yes, that's right," I say. "That's why I've never been because surfing always seems to involve some sort of ungodly hour of five o'clock in the morning."

"That's when the waves are the best," he says, spreading his arms before me as if it's the most obvious thing in the world.

"Okay. Well, when I'm not working at five in the morning, I am sleeping. There's no way I'm going into that cold ocean so early."

"What about Saturday in the afternoon when it's a high of sixty?"

"The water's still going to be crazy cold," I say.

It barely ever gets over sixty degrees. That's why I never even really go swimming in the summertime.

"C'mon, I'll get you a suit. You'll be fine if you move around."

I shake my head.

"Well, one of these days you're going to have to go."

"Oh, really?" I ask.

"Yes, really. It's something I love to do. If I'm going to be in your life, I want you to try it out."

That takes me by surprise. There's an assumption there that he wants me to be in his life.

There's an assumption there that he wants me to share something he loves. You know what? I kind of like those assumptions.

It's been a while since I've felt this seen and this wanted.

The line moves again and now it's his turn to put in an order. I ask for a latte and he asks for a cup of black coffee with nothing in it.

I insist on paying, but he refuses to accept it. I like that, too.

We don't say anything for a few minutes while we wait for the barista to make our drinks.

Then he turns to me and says, "I never answered your question."

"Which one?"

"The one from before about what I do for a living. Why I'm here."

"Yeah, that's right," I say, grabbing my cup and taking a sip.

It's warm and soothing and the burst of caffeine immediately puts me at ease. Suddenly a pang of nervousness comes on. It's difficult to explain but sometimes that happens in the afternoons right after I have my second cup of coffee of the day.

I crave it. I wait for it.

When I drink it, my body begins to tingle.

Maybe it's that or maybe it's the fact that I'm talking to Luke.

"I work for the FBI," Luke says. "I'm an agent."

“Oh…okay.”

"I'm working on a case here. It’s a joint task force."

I nod. I don't know why it feels so weird that he said that, but for some reason it does.

"Do you know Patrick?"

"Patrick Flannery?" Luke asks.

I nod.

"Yeah. He's one of my good buddies. Why?"

"I'm really good friends with his fiancée, Sydney."

"Oh, yeah. Work has been crazy this year so I haven't met her yet. I was supposed to today. We're both here on assignment."

His drink is finally ready. I'm not sure why a simple black coffee took so long, but when he grabs it, we move out of the line and toward the front door.

He takes a few steps ahead of me and opens it wide. Following him, I notice that we're both walking slowly to make this moment last a little longer.

When we get to the crosswalk, there are two uniformed officers waiting for the light.

Their radios start to blare: "Armed suspect, armed and dangerous suspect. Just robbed a bank. Headed your way on foot, southbound on Mercer and Pike."

It feels surreal. I look up at the names of the streets on the corner. We're at Mercer and Pike.

Across the street someone runs out of the bank building, fleeing with a gun in his hand. He runs up to an old beat-up station wagon.

The cops in front of us, immediately take cover behind their patrol car, open the doors, and point their weapons in his direction.

Luke and I run up to an SUV where we get a better visual on the suspect.

The suspect tries the station wagon door on one side and then on the other, but they're both locked.

I don't know if this car is his and he had just locked himself out or maybe he's just desperately trying to find a car that he can take, but he has no luck.

Kneeling down behind the SUV, I grab for my weapon and hold it steadily in one hand.

I peer over the car to see what he's doing. There's some money in a bag next to him.

When he turns toward me, I see that half of his face is covered in red, but it's not blood. It's from the dye pack that probably blew up in his face.

Two vehicles pull up, not too far away from him, just as the suspect starts loading his weapon.

He sits with his back against the station wagon.

"We have to stop him," I whisper to Luke.

He nods.

Why is he doing this? I say to myself.

"LAPD!" I yell to identify myself. "Put your hands up and no one's going to get hurt."

I don't have a megaphone, but I project as loud as I can.

"Put your hands up. You're surrounded. Do not load that weapon," I add.

The bank robber looks up startled, looking in the direction of the uniformed officers and their vehicles, probably figuring that the commands are coming from them.

"Drop the weapon!" I yell again. "Do it now."

I repeat myself multiple times, starting to feel desperate. I know what's coming if he doesn't listen, but he refuses to acknowledge me.

Time is running out.

The suspect has dirty hair and bewildered eyes. He doesn't look a day over twenty-five. He's small in stature with narrow shoulders and somewhat wide hips.

He sits with his back against the station wagon, fixated on the officers that have positioned themselves at the top of a hill. They're too far away for him to shoot, but I don't think he knows this.

He's nervous. He's afraid.

That's the worst kind of suspect to have.

At this point he's like a caged animal who will do anything to get away.

The problem is that everyone here knows that he won't.

Time starts to move in slow motion. Just like I've been taught at the police academy, I look for twitching.

I watch his body language and he appears to be disconnected from what's going on.

One moment he's nervous and out of control and the next he is calmly turning his gun cylinder one click at a time and placing bullets into each slot.

One, two, three, four.

I have to shoot him.

I have to stop him, but I still hope that he will give up he doesn't.

Instead, he snaps the drum back into place and locks it.

Now he's ready.

I don't have my radio with me, but I keep yelling out to him to surrender.

He seems to hear me and looks around, but he seems to think that the only people here are the visible ones in uniforms.

Then something changes.

"Put your hands up. You're surrounded," I say, staying careful not to allow my voice to break and to remain calm, but forceful.

Suddenly, we pass a moment of no return and then he turns into a dead man walking.

He can still surrender. He can still put down the gun and put his hands up and the cops may follow protocol. But tensions are rising.

He doesn't.

You know that moment in the movie you've seen before when you wait for some moment to come up, but it's not here yet? You know what's going to happen and you can't do anything to stop it?

This is just like that.

The suspect doesn't put his hands up. He's going to try to shoot his way out. What he doesn't know is that it won't work.

I know that he's going to die and there's not a single thing that I can do to stop it.

The suspect squats behind the car.

His elbows rest on his thighs.

He grasps the revolver with both hands as if it's his lifeline. But in reality, it's not.

The tension in his face starts to dissipate. It's like he's coming to terms with what's about to happen.

I keep hanging onto a glimmer of hope that maybe he can still live.

But then he stands up. Instead of just shooting and keeping cover, he stands up and fires a shot at the cops in the car.

He doesn't hide.

Without a second thought, everyone empties their clips into him, center mass.

This is the way we are taught to deal with armed suspects in the academy. You always shoot into the center of the chest. He knows this and it even looks like this is what he wants.

I don't know whose bullets hit him and whose don't, but a moment later, the suspect folds in half and falls onto the ground, unceremoniously and without a tinge of drama.

One moment, he's there.

The next, he's gone.

I hate the fact that he did that. I hate the fact that we all shot him. I hate the fact that I'll remember this moment for the rest of my life; the sound of the gunfire whizzing down the empty street.

For a moment, everything moves in slow motion and then the world quickly comes back.

People yell, run, check vital signs while pointing their weapons in his face.

He's been shot and he's not coming back.

Someone flips him over and we all stare at the face of the man that we shot, his face still covered in red paint from the money that he stole from the bank.

I don't know why he took it and I don't know what he meant to do with it.

I don't know why at the end, he decided to just stand up and let us take his life.

Everyone emptied their clips into him, but we did it because he wanted us to do it.

If he didn’t want this, he would have taken cover.

If he didn’t want this, he would have shot into the air.

I’ll probably never know the answers to these questions.

But Internal Affairs will definitely have a lot for me, and that's going to make it really hard to go back up to Big Bear to find my sister.

12

I see that guy when I close my eyes.

The images stay with me for a while; his body folding in half like a pair of pants at the mall, his eyes remaining open.

Luke says something to me. He touches me and yet, I can't feel him. I turn to him slowly and he mouths something.

It takes me a second to figure out what he's asking.

"Are you okay? Are you okay?"

I nod, but he doesn't take that for an answer until I say the word. We make our way over to the other officers.

Furrowed brows, clenched jaws, stern looks.

They all look at us and each other, but none of us actually focus. I slowly move my eyes from one face to another, registering, acknowledging that we are here.

Someone begins to nod and that makes it a little bit better.

An ambulance arrives.

People start to talk in louder than normal tones, but I have a hard time understanding what they're saying. The words seem to come in one ear and out the other.

My stomach feels like it's in knots, like I may throw up at any moment.

I swallow hard, inhaling a gasp of air, and then exhale very slowly, trying to calm down my beating heart.

More people show up and procedures start to take place. We have all been involved as witnesses and perpetrators.

This is a crime scene now and photos are being taken. Statements are going to be ordered next.

We're going to be put into different little rooms and questioned about what we have seen and what we haven't seen.

I know how it works.

I've never been here before, but it works pretty much the same way. Usually, the intimidating interrogation rooms are avoided and this kind of procedure takes place in the upstairs offices with big windows and broad tables.

I have to go back to the precinct. There is paperwork to fill out and statements to make, but that's the last thing I want to do.

I need to call my mom and I want to help her find Violet. Somehow thinking back to Violet puts me at ease.

Back at the precinct, there's a line of separation between the uniformed officers and the plain clothes detectives. No one talks about it, but after a few drinks, when you become a detective, there's an alienating feeling that pops up, separating you from your coworkers.

When I was a deputy, I remember the little bit of jealousy that I felt toward detectives. Part of that had to do with the normal clothes and part of that had to do with the confidence and the general air of self-assuredness that came with the title.

What I didn't know before I became a detective was all of the hours that you spend doing the work that is not particularly glamorous.

The hours spent sitting in bushes, in rain or snow.

The hours sitting in cars, eating junk food, waiting for suspects to do something to help you build your case.

Everyone involved in this shooting is wearing a uniform, except for me and Luke. We've all been sequestered in a room together and told not to talk. There are stale doughnuts and old coffee in the corner. We eat and drink even though I doubt that any of us are hungry.

The interviews proceed pretty swiftly, but hours pass before the first one begins.

There's a total of seven officers. Luke and I make nine.

When the deputies go to their meetings with Internal Affairs, the number of people slowly dwindles down until it's just me and Luke.

To try to pass the time and not talk about the case, Luke asks me about Violet. I tell him what I have found out in much more detail than I did before. He listens carefully, nodding.

A few times, he rubs the back of his head in that swift motion that shows that he's more tired than bored.

"Listen, we don't have to talk about this," I offer.

"Oh, yeah? Like what else can we talk about?"

"I don't know."

I rack my brain for something, for another possible topic of conversation, but nothing appears.

“This is the problem with socializing with people who work in law enforcement.”

Luke laughs and questions, "What do you mean?"

"Well, you know how it is. Your work is all you have to talk about."

"No, there must be other things."

"Hobbies? I’m not like you, I don’t really have any." I look at him and smile.

Our eyes meet and his glisten a little bit under the harsh fluorescent lights. He must be the only person, or at least one of a very few, who looks good under direct white light.

"Tell me about your dad," Luke says and it feels like I got punched in the stomach.

"What do you mean?" I ask, leaning on the back of the plastic chair and regretting that we haven't occupied the couch on the other side of the room.

Now, even though there are only two of us left here, it feels odd to suddenly get up and move.

"I don't know. You just never mentioned him before. I was wondering why."

I bite the inside of my cheek. I don't know whether sitting in this waiting room with a guy that I've had barely two dates with is the right time to talk about my father.

"Things have been complicated," I say. "I don't really like talking about it."

"Oh, okay," he says with a nod. "I understand."

I doubt that, I want to say, but I don't want to be rude.

"So, what's your plan for Violet? Did your mom put out the flyers?"

"No, not yet. I guess I should have told her to do them today. Uh, I don't know," I say.

Burying my fingers in my hair, I realize just how greasy it is and hate the fact that I haven't had the chance to spray it with dry shampoo.

"I'm going to text her to get those printed and start plastering them everywhere…" I let my words hang there.

I don't know how to finish the sentence. I don't know how to deal with all of the hundreds of thoughts milling around in my mind seemingly all at once.

"If you don't want to talk about Violet, it's fine. I don't want to pressure you."

"No, it's not that. It's just... It's everything. It's just too much, this shooting, the Reynard girl, Violet. Doesn't it feel like this job is just too much sometimes?"

"Yeah, it does." Luke nods.

Leaning on his knees, he props his arms up to support his head and looks up.

His hair falls slightly in his face. He looks so beautiful and handsome with those high cheekbones and the strong jawline.

Yet, he also looks vulnerable and real all at the same time.

"I like you," he says.

Just like that.

No pretense.

No qualifiers.

"I like you, too," I say, tilting my head just a little bit, staring deep into his eyes.

I bite my lower lip.

I move a little bit closer to him and then he kisses me, pressing his lips tightly against mine. They're soft and yet strong. He kisses me and then pulls me closer to him.

My hands make their way around his neck and into his hair. This is the first thing, the first good thing that I've felt in a long time.

Just before we separate, the door to the room
swings open and a uniformed officer whose name
I don't know tells me to follow him.

13

Nobody wants to be assigned to the Internal Affairs Division, IAD. In fact, it's usually referred to as the kiss of death.

Internal Affairs investigate officers for anything that's considered to be acts of treason. Everyone who has ever watched any television show knows that there is a silent and unspoken code among cops that creates the solid bond between these men and women in blue.

Cops are ganged and their membership is incredibly loyal. Police officers will fight, lie, and cheat for one another.

If you say something against one of them, they can be pretty vindictive and vengeful. I know this as I walk over to the room where they're going to conduct my interview.

Usually, Internal Affairs doesn't handle this kind of situation. This is just an officer-involved shooting but given what has been going on recently around the country, an IAD will be at this interrogation.

We walk down a long hallway and go into a big, wide room with enormous windows looking out onto the city below.

Captain Medvil sits at one end of the table and introduces two IAD officers to me whom I've only seen briefly walking down the halls.

There are two other sergeants in the room as well. They are all here to judge, analyze, and interpret my version of events. No one ever wants to be involved in IAD investigations. In order to lessen the animosity toward these investigators, the Chief of Police tends to rotate detectives through the IAD department.

Everybody is cordial and polite. The friendliness that I have had with Captain Medvil before is gone.

The row of men, and I do mean men, sit across from me with folders in front of them, the contents of which are a mystery to me.

"Tell us what happened," Captain Medvil says.

I start at the beginning.

I tell them every detail that I can remember.

I pause on a few and reiterate.

"He stood up," I say. "He had the gun. He shot at the other officers. He never responded to any of my attempts to get him to step down."

Their faces are blank.

They reveal nothing, but I know what happened. Unlike many other officer-involved shootings, this case is pretty black and white.

Everyone knows that he had a gun. A few people saw it get loaded and he didn't respond to anyone trying to get him to step down.

This is a classic textbook case of suicide by cop, where the suspect shoots at the officers, knowing that he's going to get killed.

After they listen to my whole story, it's time for me to ask a question.

"Do you think you'll be able to find any businesses that have a recording of what happened? There must have been some cameras pointed in this direction or maybe even some news people from the helicopters above."

"Some of the videos have been retrieved already," Captain Medvil says. "They seem to align to what you said."

"Good, good. This was a very unfortunate incident," I say. "I'm just sorry that it happened at all. It shouldn't have."

The officer on the other side of Captain Medvil who read me my Miranda Rights, informed me of my right to department grievance procedures, and my right to have an attorney present, writes down something frivolously in his notebook.

I wonder what it could be and whether or not it affects this case at all. Then, when it's almost time for me to go, he looks up, narrowing his eyes.

He has a standard issue haircut and the broad stance used to exhibit authority and impose it on others.

He's the kind of cop that I don't like because I can't tell if he actually thinks that he knows everything that he needs to know or if he is just putting on a show.

"I hate to say this," I add, almost as an afterthought, "but I kind of got the sense that that guy wanted to die. I mean, I know that he'd just robbed a bank, but sometimes you see it on their faces. It's like one wrong thing happened after another, and another and he just couldn't bear it. He just couldn't deal with the possibility of going to jail. I don't know anything about him or his record and I don't know if he's been to prison before, but sometimes it's the people who haven't been there who are the most scared."

"Thank you for your time, Detective Carr," Captain Medvil says. "We will be in touch."

"Oh, one more thing." The guy next to him stands up just as I'm about to leave.

I turn around to face them and see the way that he leans over the oak table and looks up from his notes.

"You said that you emptied your clip, right?" There's a cockiness to the voice like he's challenging me with something that he knows isn't true.

"Um, I don't know about emptying my clip, but I shot him just like everyone else did."

"No, you didn't," he says.

I glance down at his name tag, Officer Delinsky. Now, I'm sure that I will remember his name.

"I don't know what you're talking about."

"Well, Detective Carr, with all due respect."

I clench my jaw. "With all due respect" is one of those lines that people use whenever they are just about to disrespect you.

I wait for him to continue.

"You surrendered your weapon and we had the forensics team go through it. No bullets were used. Apparently, you never even discharged it."

"What are you talking about?" I ask, unfolding my hands and staring at him in disbelief. "I was there. I shot him along with everyone else."

"No, you didn't," Captain Medvil says, shaking his head. "You're just a witness. You identified yourself and told him to stand down. Everyone confirmed that. But you, in fact, did not shoot him."

The words hit me like a gust of wind. They collide with me and then go through me.

I don't understand what they are saying to me. How could I have not shot him?

I was so certain that I had my gun in my hand. I had it extended in front of me.

I remember pointing it at him and then that's when the shooting started, but, of course, the explosion of gunfire sounds like firecrackers and I guess none of them came from me.

"It's fine, Detective Carr. You did nothing wrong," Captain Medvil says. "We just thought that you should know that you actually did not shoot him."

I nod and walk out of the meeting hall with my head hanging low.

I feel the slope of my shoulders and straighten them out just before the door closes behind me.

I make my way down the hallway and all the way downstairs to the locker room. That's finally when I collapse.

I sit on the toilet and I let all of the stress and the emotion of the day flow out of me. I hate the tears.

I hate the fact that men can just channel all of that stress and frustration into anger, but I never can.

I don't cry often, but today, it's just too much. I'm overwhelmed and out of control, but a few strong gasps and purposeful breathing exercises finally start to relax me.

I dry my tears with toilet paper, put in my AirPods, and turn on my favorite meditation app.

Five minutes of the soothing voice and the calming presence focuses my thinking and puts me back in the driver's seat of my life. When I walk back out to wash my hands, I feel like a new woman.

14

I change into a pair of comfortable jeans and a loose fitting blouse, professional, but not so dressed up like the pencil skirt that I had on before.

It's getting late now, but I still have work to do. I head to my desk and open the computer. I check my phone, and then text my mom with a template to create the missing poster for Violet.

It contains all the basic information: white female,110 pounds, 5'4", 13 years old, brown eyes, brown hair, last seen…

I have seen plenty of these missing posters in my career, but I've never thought that my sister would be on one of them.

There are big, red letters with the word *MISSING* at the top. I need my mom to attach three recent photographs.

Just as I'm about to text her this information, I just do it myself. I know my sister's social media and I know which pictures will look the most like her and be most appropriate for the poster.

I go to Instagram, her preferred platform, and see that she hasn't posted any stories since a day ago. Usually, she doesn't miss one and I like getting these updates.

Even though we don't talk on the phone very often, it's nice to see her and her life in this lens. I never had that myself growing up and I wonder what kind of stuff I would have posted and what kind of persona I would have been online as a teenager because that's what we are after all.

We are projections of ourselves.

We show the world what we want to be like and even those people who show themselves with all their flaws and all are carefully curating their imperfect lives.

Looking through my sister's Instagram with a more investigative eye rather than a big sister eye like I did before, I notice a few things. There are very few pictures of her and her friends.

Most images are selfies or pictures of sunsets, snow, and animals. Man, she loves animals.

I do, too. I remember how much I used to beg my mom to get me a cat or a dog, but she never relented. It's the same way with my sister.

For some reason, my mom has always been very anti-pets and I wish that I could give my sister a pet or even have one for myself, but I work too many hours and it would be unfair.

I click on a few photos on which some of her friends are tagged and I look at their innocent faces. I wonder what secrets they are holding deep within their souls.

Thirteen year olds always have secrets.

I look up Kaylee's Instagram and unlike Violet's, hers is dominated by filters, selfies, cars, and pretty much anything else. In half of the pictures, she doesn't even look like the real girl. I guess that's the point.

I type in Neil Goss's name and look through a string of various guys before spotting him at the very bottom.

He has 5,000 friends, a high number for a middle school kid who isn't Instagram famous.

I notice that most of the pictures were taken either by a friend or by a tripod, a little bit further away than a selfie arm can reach. They're usually torso or full-body shots of him playing hockey, him playing basketball, him playing video games.

He's confident about his looks because, well, he looks like he's at least three years older and has the attitude of a cool thirty-year-old. This is the kind of kid who would probably do well in Hollywood. I can definitely see him on daytime television.

Neil's Instagram doesn't reveal anything off the bat, but I write down the names of a few people that he has tagged and search their Instagrams as well. I'm well aware of the fact that there's now Snapchat, TikTok, and other platforms that I have to check.

I don't exactly know what I'm looking for, but I have a feeling that this would be the place to find it. I still have the hope that maybe Violet is with someone from school.

Why would she be with someone from school and not tell my mom about it?

Did something happen between the two of them or maybe I'm off track altogether?

Maybe someone grabbed her and took her somewhere and this person is a complete stranger.

This is, of course, the worst-case scenario. These are the type of cases that are practically impossible to solve because there's very little evidence showing you who could've done it until the body shows up.

When the phrase *the body* rushes through my mind, I get goose bumps up and down my arms.

No, I can't think like that.

No, my sister cannot be *the body*. She cannot be the victim.

I cannot think, I cannot let myself think in those terms.

There must be something else here that I'm missing. I keep searching before going on to Snapchat and TikTok, the platforms that I'm least familiar with.

I decide to try my hand at Facebook. I don't even know if Violet has one anymore, except for to log into various other websites, but when I check it, I'm pleasantly surprised.

She does have one and she has recently been active. In fact, an hour before Kaylee and her mom dropped her off, she posted something.

"I'll see you soon."

I furrow my brow.

"I'll see you soon?"

The name that appears at the top is Briana Moody. I click on it, but there's no picture.

The profile seems blank. It either was blank all along or someone had recently deleted it and all of its contents.

I write down the name and repeat it a few times so it becomes familiar, like something I've known all along.

I find a few pictures of Violet from her Instagram that show her in the most natural way, hair down, no filters, and the normal amount of makeup that she typically wears.

I attach them to the missing poster that I then print out on the computer.

We're not supposed to use the printer for mass mailings, but I make twenty-five copies and then send the poster as a PDF to my mom's email.

I know that she doesn't check her messages often, so I text her, "Get these printed and distribute them all over town. I'll be up tonight or tomorrow morning and I'll help you."

I send the PDF to Captain Talarico as well and he surprises me by getting back to me right away with, "Thank you. Give me a call when you can."

I do so, immediately.

"That's a good poster that you made," he says.

His voice sounds gruff and harsh on the other end like he needs to clear his throat.

"Are you back in town?"

"No, I still have work to do here in LA, but I'll try to get back as soon as I can."

I don't want him to abandon the investigation or just think that she left on her own, but at the same time, they are searching for her and I need them to know everything that they can.

"Briana Moody," I say.

"Is that supposed to mean anything?"

"I checked Violet's Facebook and an hour before she got dropped off at home, she posted on Briana Moody's wall that she can't wait to see her soon. I don't know who she is. There're no pictures. There's no other information. I can try to find her to see if she has an Instagram account or some other social media, but I basically don't even know who I'm looking for."

"Okay. Have you talked to Kaylee about it?"

"No, I haven't." I shake my head even though he can't see me.

I play with the little string on my desk lamp. It's one of those old-fashioned ones that used to be popular in law firms all around the country. I'm tempted to pull down on it and turn it on and off, but I don't want to bother my fellow desk mates.

"I'm going to ask people about that."

"Hmm."

"I guess try to find out who Briana Moody is. That's a big piece of evidence that could really help," he says.

"Were you able to find anything on her computer?"

He doesn't respond at first.

"Captain Talarico?"

"Um, yeah, we were able to find something," he says, taking time between words as if he is biting his tongue.

"What is it?" I ask.

15

Captain Talarico's hiding something. Well, maybe not hiding, but definitely avoiding.

I press him again and again and finally he says, "Your sister's computer had a lot of interesting information on it."

He pauses at the word interesting to cast some judgement, but I wait for him to continue. I need to know more.

"What do you mean?"

"Well, there were a lot of images."

"What do you mean? Like pictures?"

"Yes."

"Of what?"

"Of *her*."

My heart sinks.

"Doing what?"

"A lot of things," he says.

I don't know him well. Actually, not at all and I can't tell if he's just trying to be polite or if this is actually making him uncomfortable.

"Please, you have to tell me what's going on."

“There are images. Mostly of other kids at her school. Many of them are quite artistic with filters, black and white and distorted. That kind of thing. Almost all of them are nude."

I ball up my fists.

“It’s not the best, but also pretty common."

Back when I was growing up, cameras weren’t so common and it took a lot of effort to snap nude photos of yourself.

That is not the case anymore. Now with cameras being installed onto every single iPhone, teenagers can take millions of pictures of themselves in all sorts of poses, dressed and undressed.

The department has had hundreds of cases involving young adults basically making underage pornography without even knowing it.

"These are a little different," the captain says. "There are videos of a few different guys and a few different girls. We're still in the process of identifying everybody. I'm not sure if this is related to her disappearance or why she was keeping all of these images on her computer, but it's something that we need to go through."

"I'd like to see them," I say.

"Yes, of course. Maybe you can even help us identify some of the kids, but we cannot send them out. You have to come here. Chain of evidence, you know."

"Yes, of course," I say. "I'll be there tomorrow morning at the latest."

I stare at the phone after I hang up, not certain of what this means or what I have to do now. The way that he had talked about the videos makes me uneasy.

I haven't lived with Violet for years, but I never got the sense that she was the hard partying kind or a social butterfly or the kind of girl who uses her sexuality to get attention.

Violet always seemed to be the complete opposite of that. The videos and the fact that she has been storing them on her laptop are both concerns.

It could be something innocent or it could be something that comes back to haunt her.

Or it could have something to do with this case.

Teens don't realize that if you make a threat that you're going to release the video in order to get something that you want is called blackmail. Blackmail is against the law.

There's so much more that I don't know about my sister and suddenly I feel like I hardly knew her at all.

In order to take my mind off of Violet and all of these unknowns, I focus on what I do know. I turn my attention to Courtney Reynard's preliminary medical examiner report, going through it carefully.

Evidence of strangulation

"Duh, of course," I say, thinking back to the rope and how that girl was hanging off that tree before the dog walker cut her down.

Evidence of blunt force trauma

This means that she must've been hit by something, but what and why?

I call the ME on the phone and I talk to her about her findings. Since she does a number of these every day, it takes her a little bit to find the report.

"So, you think that this is definitely *not* suicide?" I ask to confirm what I already suspect.

"No, definitely not. The blunt force trauma explains that the victim couldn’t have gotten herself onto that tree by herself. There's no ladder, right?"

“No.” I shake my head.

Dr. Laura Berinsky is sharp. Nothing gets past her.

"What do you think happened?" I ask. "What does the evidence tell you?"

"The simplest explanation is probably someone hit her on the head, she lost consciousness, and he hung her. She was still alive when the hanging happened, so she suffocated. It took a long time."

"Really?" I ask with a gasp.

It hadn't occurred to me.

"I was so certain that she... I thought that maybe her neck snapped,” I suggest. “I heard that happens during a hanging."

"Yeah. That happens when you do a hanging properly like they used to for executions. But if you don't fall far enough, your neck doesn't snap. In this case, he just hung her by the noose and she suffocated.”

I put my hand over my mouth in shock. "How long do you think it took her to die?"

"I don't know. A few minutes, maybe five, seven. It took a while. I don't know if that guy stood there and watched her, but he's one sick creep."

I exhale and suddenly have a strong urge to take a shower.

"How could he have done that to her? Why?" I ask. The questions are more rhetorical than anything.

"I have no idea. That's your job, Kaitlyn," she jokes.

"You know, on television, people like you seem to do all the work for me," I say with a laugh.

She laughs and I hear her baby cry out in the background.

"How's Timothy doing?"

"Good, good. A bit colicky. These three-hour feedings are really getting to be a lot," Laura says. "I thought that he'd be sleeping more through the night now that he's almost five months, but no luck here. He's awake and ready to party and hungry all the time."

"I don't know how you do this, work full-time and take care of a baby by yourself."

After years of bad luck with flaky men, she took matters into her own hands and got pregnant through a sperm donor.

"Hey, women do it all the time, right?"

"Let me know if you need any help whatsoever."

"With what? The case or my baby?"

I hesitate, considering my options. "I guess I'm more likely to solve the case but I'm available to babysit if you need me."

"Yeah, no, I'm good." She chuckles.

I can almost see her tossing her caramel hair and throwing her arms up in protest.

"Hey, what is that supposed to mean?" I ask sarcastically, pretending to be confused or insulted.

"You know exactly what it means. You and kids. I don't know, maybe it'll work out when you have your own, but I'm not using mine as a guinea pig."

We both laugh and I know that she's right.

"Okay. Well, if you have any other information for me, get in touch," I say and hang up.

Taking a break, I head to the vending machine for a bag of pretzels. This is my go-to snack whenever I need a little pick-me-up. I know that I should be eating something healthier like an apple, but in this line of work, you'll take any comfort that you can get. I'm just glad that I don't stuff my face full of Krispy Kreme donuts every morning like some people do.

After popping a few into my mouth and washing them down with ice cold water, my thoughts drift back to Laura. She is three years older than I am and yet I'm as far as I can get from entertaining the thought of having children of my own.

For many years, I never gave it any thought.

I was never one of those women who ever wanted children right from the start. I never planned a wedding. I never planned anything in my life except for going to college and then to the police academy.

Now I wonder if maybe I do want to have a child. Maybe it is time and maybe I should think about it before it's too late.

Of course, before I do that, I have to have a boyfriend, or do I?

Laura doesn't.

Laura got divorced two years ago from a man who told her three years into their marriage that he never wanted to have children.

So, she went to the sperm bank. She has a babysitter to help her out when she's working, but most of the time, she's on her own.

Can I do that?

Can I take care of a baby all on my own? I mean, of course it's physically possible and I know that lots of women do it and have done it over the years, but I just can't imagine myself in that position.

Besides, I've never thought of myself as the motherly type. I guess I could blame my mom, right? Can't we just blame our parents for everything?

In this case, I don't know if she fits the bill. She's the one who's always been asking me about when I'm finally going to have a child.

I sit down at my desk again and open my laptop to read Laura's report in more detail, but I can't focus.

I turn my attention to something else instead. I click on Facebook and look through my old friends' happy families. Some have big houses, others have pretty small apartments, but everyone is smiling and sharing their lives with the families they've created now.

That's what happens, right?

You get to a certain point and when someone asks, 'how is so-and-so?' the answer is always well, *they're married*, and they have children or at least a child.

I don't even have a plan.

I don't even have a pet.

I don't even have a plant.

Something about that makes me smirk and laugh. While I did recently get a fig tree, but whether or not it makes it long term, I have no idea. I have not had the best luck in growing plants and have them survive and thrive for more than a month or two.

Hostile home environment? Perhaps.

Then for some reason, I type *his* name into the search bar.

Luke Gavinson.

I know his last name now. I looked it up. FBI agent. He doesn't put that on his Facebook profile.

No, here are just pictures of him playing football, laughing with friends, and swimming in a pool.

I zoom in.

His abs glisten as he jumps out of the water to hit a ball over the net. I make the picture a little bit bigger to get a better visual.

Wow, I say to myself. I mean, I felt them under the clothes, but do they actually *look* like this?

Something inside of me stirs. It's that familiar feeling that reminds me that despite all of my cerebral thoughts, I'm an animal after all with urges, needs, and unfulfilled desires.

"Hey." His voice startles me.

When Luke's hand lands on my shoulder, I practically jump out of my seat, spilling and knocking over my open bottle of water.

"Oh my God. I'm so sorry," he says, jumping up to pick up the bottle and clean up some of the damage.

The water floods all over, all around the laptop, but luckily he picks it up in time. Luke picks it up fast enough to prevent any major damage.

"You really scared me," I say in a huff, holding my stomach, trying to calm down my beating heart.

"Look at this," Luke says, staring at the screen. "You were looking me up."

My cheeks turn bright red.

I can feel the heat emanating from them and I want to do something to make all of this go away, but I can't.

He's standing right before me holding my open laptop to a zoomed in picture of his abs.

No, no, no. Make this go away.

"I don't know. I just looked you up and..." I mumble something, turning my face away from him.

He puts my laptop carefully on a nearby desk and grabs a roll of paper towels to help me clean up the puddle.

"You were looking me up," Luke says, smiling at the corner of his lips.

"Okay. So, I was looking you up," I admit, rushing my words and rubbing every last drop of water from the table while avoiding eye contact.

"So, did you like what you saw?"

"If you're going to get a big head about it, then your abs are only going to carry you so far."

"You want to see them in real life?"

"No, I don't," I say, tugging on his shirt to pull it back down after he tries to raise it. "We're at work."

He looks around the room. We're all alone.

The lights are dim and my lamp is one of the few ones on.

I pull another sheet off of the roll and press it to the last of the water. He pulls his hand over mine and I feel how warm and comforting it is.

I let go of the paper towel and let our fingers intertwine.

I look up at him.

Then he presses his lips to mine. When my mouth opens, our breaths become one. He pulls me closer to him and I feel the hardness of his body against mine.

I stand on my tiptoes and I kiss him again and again. He kisses me back.

His hands make their way up and down my back. I suddenly feel incredibly safe and turned on all at once.

He buries his fingers in my hair, twirling around his fingers and sending shivers down my back.

We stand in this moment for as long as we can.

Then Luke pulls away and asks, "Do you want to come over?"

I nod and he kisses me again.

16

After a night of lovemaking, I wake up super early having barely had an hour and a half of shut eye. As soon as I lift my heavy eyelids, I see Luke's face in front of me, eyes closed, relaxed, at peace.

I look at his lips and remember all of the places that they were last night and how that made me feel.

"Hey, you're awake," he says, startling me.

"Huh? Yeah, I guess."

Luke leans over and gives me a little peck on my cheek.

"Last night was something," he says in that casual tone of his that makes me forget my own name.

"Yeah, it was," I say, pulling away but keeping the sheet tight around my body.

"What are you doing?"

His hands make their way up and down my body, first over the sheet, and then sliding underneath.

"No, I can't," I mumble.

"You can't or you don't want to?"

"I can't. I wish that I could."

I have a three-hour drive ahead of me if I want to get there before school starts to talk to Natalie.

When Luke pulls away from me, I watch the way the faint morning light emphasizes every muscle in his arms.

"You get a good look?" he asks, tilting his head back.

"I wasn't even looking at you," I lie through my teeth.

"Yeah, right…I actually have to head to the airport soon."

“Where are you going?”

“Stockton. There's a case that my boss is thinking of assigning me to. I'm not really sure about the details. I should be back in a couple of days, I hope."

“Me, too," I say, picking my clothes up off the floor.

"Can I make you breakfast?" Luke offers, heading to the kitchen.

"No, I don't have time. I don't know how long it's going to take me to go up the hill. Weather might be bad, so can the traffic. The sooner I get going, the better."

"Got it.”

After getting dressed, I cake my hair in dry shampoo, brush it out, and apply a little bit of eyeliner and makeup.

I want to jump into the shower, but I'm afraid that I'll be late.

Instead, I grab my bag and wave good-bye. When I start to walk away from him, Luke grabs my hand and pulls me close to him.

"I had a really good time last night," he whispers.

Our faces are so close that our noses are touching.

I can smell the minty freshness of his newly brushed teeth.

"Can we do it again sometime?" he asks.

I want to say no.

I promised myself that I was no longer going to get involved with anyone in law enforcement, but Luke gives me that look that makes me remember our time together and how much he made me laugh.

"Call me later," I say, "or text."

"I'll call," he promises.

I smile, not wanting to pull my hand away from him.

I'm glad that he'll call instead of text.

I reach over to him and give him one last kiss.

"Talk to you later," he says when I finally pull away.

"I'll be looking forward to it." I laugh and so does he.

Walking out of his apartment, I have a big, wide grin on my face that I can't remove.

Surprisingly, the drive to Big Bear takes only two hours as there's very little traffic and the mountain road is free of accidents and tourists.

Four in the morning is the best time to leave LA, I say to myself. Not wanting to waste time, I head straight to Natalie's house.

Natalie D'Achille lives in an upper middle-class neighborhood in the newly developed part of Big Bear, at the outskirts. I found her mom's address online.

The houses here are contemporary, all built in the last ten years or so and resemble what you would call McMansions. They are about 2,500 to 3,000 square foot, three to four bedrooms each with two-car garages.

Her house sits at the end of a cul-de-sac in a cookie-cutter community of at least forty other houses. Personally, I wouldn't mind living in a place like this. I've always liked the idea of old houses, the character and the detail, but after having lived in one for years and then lived in an older apartment for years as an adult, I've realized that their character is really a big headache.

There are always things breaking. There are always pipes leaking and sewage getting built up.

The house that I grew up in has had numerous leaks through the ceiling from various snowstorms, as well as problems with rodents and broken heaters.

I used to think it was just my house, but after talking to a few friends, I realized that this problem is so much more common than I ever thought.

As much as I used to look down on people who would move into these cookie-cutter communities when I was a teenager, now I sort of want a house here with tall ceilings, good lighting, relatively modern fixtures, well-sealed against heat, bugs, and the cold, with no worries about the snow ever getting in or the pipes freezing up.

I get to Natalie's house right around six thirty and I know that my presence there will be a surprise. That's partly the goal, but still, I'd be lying if I didn't say that I was a little bit nervous.

The thing is that I'm not a natural at interviewing people, let alone interrogation. I'm not great at confrontations and I think that what makes me such an effective detective is that people sense that and they connect with me.

I can get people to open up because I'm pushy when I have to be and I'm not when I feel the situation is changing.

I park my car a little bit down the block and walk up the pristine, freshly manicured street. The lawns here are big, wide, very green, and probably recently seeded.

The snow has all but melted and it's going to be a warm day in the seventies. The sky is already bright blue and filling my mind with optimism for all of the things that could happen.

I've always reacted this way to weather. That's one of the reasons why I like living in LA. It puts my mind at ease. The sunny days bring brightness to my life and anytime there's any sort of bad weather, gray clouds, or even a little bit of rain, I feel my mood shifting, becoming more introverted, internal, and dark.

I double-check Natalie's address on my phone before knocking on the door, using their big brass knocker. There's a camera installed and I'm certain someone is looking at my face right about now. I smile and look as friendly as possible.

A few minutes later, a woman in her forties, not that much older than I am, opens the door. Her hair is tied up in a towel and she's wearing a bathrobe.

"May I help you?"

I introduce myself, making sure to name-check the LAPD to give myself a little bit more authority when I really don't have any. "May I speak to your daughter, Natalie D'Achille?"

"Oh my God, why?" Her mom gasps, clutching her silk bathrobe, the kind that I thought people only wore in movies. "Does she need a lawyer?"

"No, no, no. She hasn't done anything wrong. My sister's missing. I'm looking for her. They go to school together. They're in the same grade, Violet Carr."

I wait for her to register the name and to either nod or shake her head, whether she has heard it, but she does neither.

She just stands there, staring, looking somewhere behind me.

"I'm sorry to bother you again," I apologize, "but I just wanted to ask her a few questions about where she was that night and whether maybe she was with her or ..."

"Okay. Well, I guess there's no problem with that," she says. "Come on in."

I nod and cross the threshold. She tells me to wait in the foyer as she goes upstairs and yells for her daughter.

A few minutes later, two boys come down the stairs. They run and skip two steps at a time. They don't notice me until they nearly tumble over me.

"Hi, my name is Detective Carr. I was wondering if you happen to know my sister, Violet, Violet Carr?"

"Oh, yeah," one of them says. He's the one with the thicker jowls and the narrower eyes. He introduces himself as Michael. "Yeah, I have art class with Violet."

"On the night of the eighteenth, she never came home," I launch right in. "She was supposed to get in by nine and she never did. Her friend Kaylee and her mom dropped her off, but she never got inside, so I'm just trying to ask her friends and anyone who may know her if they might have heard her say that she was meeting up with someone or had any other plans, something that she might not have told Kaylee about."

They exchange looks and purse their lips, shaking their heads.

I wait for them to elaborate, but they just shrug and I figure that the conversation is over.

A few minutes later, Natalie comes downstairs.

She has long, blonde hair and expertly applied makeup. She looks just like the most popular girl at school looked like when I was her age, confident, aware of her body, and most importantly aware of the way that other people see her.

I introduce myself and review what I have previously told her brothers. They're all triplets, born the same day, but they could not look less alike.

Natalie looks like she is at least two years older and acts like she's a decade older than her brothers.

She holds her chin up high and her shoulders are broad, exuding confidence.

That is rare at this age, especially when talking to detectives. As a police officer, I've been taught to notice things; pay attention to the details, and the minutia of life that other people don't see.

As a homicide detective, paying attention to these things has made me particularly good at my job.

Like, for example, I know that people treat me completely different when they meet me in the streets with my hair tied up in a loose bun, wearing leggings, and acting like any other woman in her thirties, obsessed with her phone.

When I come to them in the capacity of my job with my badge in hand, there's a separateness that is created. There's a casualness that disappears.

I guess that's to be expected, except that I didn't realize just how informally they had previously treated me. Before, they knew what I really did for a living, but when it comes to Natalie, I don't feel this difference in attitude.

My job title and my purpose in being here doesn't seem to faze her at all.

I don't know yet if this is just for show or her normal way of being, but I take note.

For a little bit of privacy, I pull her away into the dining room. It's simple in design, but the table is wide and beautiful.

Come to think of it, I've seen it in the pages of a Pottery Barn catalog. "I wanted to ask you about the night of the eighteenth. Can you tell me where you were that night?"

"I don't know, here. I don't remember doing anything special that night."

"You were here. Who were you with?"

"Ah." She tilts her head back and thinks for a moment. "I don't know. Actually, I was here by myself. My brothers had hockey practice and I was here. Did some homework, watched some Netflix. I don't know, just a regular evening, I guess."

"You didn't go out anywhere? What about around ten at night?"

"Nope, still here. I think I went to bed early. I was really tired. I'd had a test earlier that day."

I nod. It is not lost on me the fact that she and Neil have different stories.

I wasn't sure what I was going to find out coming to Natalie's house but this contradiction takes me by surprise.

Why would Neil, her boyfriend, say that they were together the night of the eighteenth, especially around ten p.m., but she says that they weren't?

She may not want her mom or her brothers to know, but we're alone here in this room. They are somewhere in the kitchen talking loudly and clearly not eavesdropping.

I pull Natalie closer to the window.

"Please, don't feel like you ... I don't want to make you uncomfortable, but you have to tell me the truth. I'm not going to tell your brothers or your mom or anyone, but I have to know. What were you doing the night of the eighteenth?"

This frankness and the clear urgency in my voice seems to take her by surprise. She loses her composure for a moment. The expression on her face falls and she doesn't look like the confident, outgoing little girl that she was just a little bit ago.

"I'm really sorry about Violet," she says.

"Yes, please help me find her."

"I don't know what I can say. I have no idea where she is."

"Can you just tell me ..."

The conversation is drifting off course. I don't want her to think that I'm accusing her of anything, but I need her to tell me the truth.

"Please tell me what you were doing that night exactly."

She takes a pause.

She thinks about it and I can tell something different about this delivery. There's more honesty to it, but not fake honesty, not performative honesty. She shifts her weight from one foot to another, crosses and uncrosses her arms.

Finally, she raises her eyes and meets my gaze.

"I was home all night. I'm not sure if someone told you something different, but this is where I was. I had plans to go out with Neil, but I didn't. I was just too tired. I had a test and I was going to do some homework. I was going to start on a project that I was totally supposed to start about two weeks before and of course I didn't."

"So, you were home all night. What about your family? Were they here also?"

"Yeah, my brothers got home around eight and then we ordered some pizza, stayed in, and I think I went to bed around ten, kind of early for me but like I said, I was really tired."

I debate with myself whether I should reveal the fact that Neil had told me something else, but I decide to keep that in my back pocket for now.

After her brothers confirm her story, I head toward the door with more questions than answers, turning around right before I grab the doorknob.

"Oh, one more thing." I turn to Natalie.

"Yes?"

"Do you know who Briana Moody is?"

She looks at me with a blank face, and a confused look.

I spell her name and wait for some sort of connection, but she shakes her head.

"The name doesn't sound familiar at all?" I press.

"Nope, sorry."

"Okay, well, thank you for your time," I say, walking out.

Her phone goes off and she looks at the screen right as I step outside onto the porch.

The last thing I see before she closes the door is that the call is from Neil Goss.

I get back in the car and wait a few minutes. Maybe she'll run after me, tell me something that she hasn't said yet. I'm certain that Natalie's going to tell Neil about our little conversation.

I'm sure that she'll tell him about my stopping by and the questioning. I wonder how the conversation about their conflicting stories is going to go.

Frankly, I have no idea which one of them is telling me the truth. I knew that Neil was full of it when I first met him, but that doesn't mean that every single thing that he told me is a lie.

Yet this morning, I got the clear impression that Natalie was telling me the truth.

That means Neil was lying, but why?

I decide to give him a call. Perhaps the best thing to do is to just catch him unaware and get him to confess or admit something that he wouldn't if he had some time to think about it.

It goes straight to voice mail.

I know that he must have looked at the screen, saw that it was me, and ignored it.

I'm tempted to leave a message, but I don't.

Instead, I get back on the road and start driving in search of coffee.

A few minutes later, my phone rings. It's Neil.

17

"Hey, how are you?" I say, answering the phone in my most friendly and peppy voice. "Thanks for calling me back."

"I'm not supposed to talk to you," Neil says.

"So, thanks for calling me back," I repeat myself. "I just wanted to ask you why you told me that you were with your girlfriend Natalie when you weren't on the night of the eighth?"

"Yes, I was."

"No, no, you weren't. Not according to her."

He pauses, hesitates. Now I know something is up.

"Listen, I just talked to her and she didn't say anything about it," he admits.

This takes me by surprise.

I was so certain that two thirteen year olds who recently talked to an LAPD detective would at least discuss that incident with each other. Or maybe he's just lying.

"So, can you tell me what you were doing on the night of the eighteenth?" I ask. "The truth this time."

I hear him hesitating. I can almost imagine him licking his lips and opening his mouth to say something, but then stopping himself.

"My parents told me that you have to go through our lawyer and that I can't talk to you anymore. I'm sorry about that," he says and hangs up, just like that, click and the conversation's over.

I wait at the red light and look at my black screen.

Neil and Natalie have exuded more confidence and self-assuredness talking to me than most grown adults have. They may not know this but this gives them the ability to wield a lot of power. They have the ability to get away with anything. Perhaps, they already have.

I keep driving down Big Bear Boulevard, past my mom's house and the Village. The road veers off and I follow it into Whispering Pines toward the Goss's house.

I shouldn’t do this, but I have to try. Yes, he hung up on me, but perhaps in person he won't be able to be so dismissive.

I drive up to the gate, press the intercom, and wait for someone to answer. I keep calling and then after a few rings someone comes on, a voice that I don't recognize.

"Please leave us alone, Detective Carr. We have nothing else to say to you. You can now go and get all of your questions answered through our attorney."

The voice is practically robotic in its delivery, but it is not a recording. It belongs to a woman, but not his mother. It doesn’t sound familiar.

I mutter to myself and turn around in the driveway right before the gate.

It's a relatively tight fit and it takes me a few turns to get out.

I DEBATE what to do next. Maybe I should go see my mom and check on those flyers or go to Violet’s school. There is a lot to do, but suddenly I can’t bring myself to do anything.

I feel lost and alone.

I need my sister back.

I haven't had much sleep and my emotional breaking point isn't as far removed as I usually like it to be. I've always been this way about sleep.

If I don't get enough shut-eye, I can get triggered by any number of things and most have nothing to do with what's going on.

Many men in my line of work are the same way but instead of tears they yell or throw a punch or discharge their weapon. Due to an unfortunate double standard, getting angry isn't considered a weakness, but getting sad is.

"I need some coffee," I say to myself and drive over to the Starbucks in the main shopping plaza in front of the Ralph's.

There's a Radio Shack across the street along with the Dollar General where I used to shop for all sorts of little finds. I've always liked flea markets and 99 cent stores and anywhere you can get a deal.

Big department stores have everything, but it's places like this where you find something you wouldn't expect. The inventory is constantly changing. One week they have something, the next they don't, and you never know what you're going to find.

After getting a latte and enjoying the first surge of caffeine through my veins, I walk over to the dollar store and meander through the aisles, picking up a few of the items.

When I get to the candy aisle, I can't stop myself. Dark chocolate is my kryptonite. I love it. The darker, the better.

On this particular occasion, they happened to have some 88% and I grab the Midnight Blue Bar for just a dollar.

I'm chewing on the first square before I even get back to the car and I haven't even had breakfast yet. I know that my chocolate addiction is not something that's ever going to help me lose those fifteen pounds, but I'm not starting any new diets today. What I need now is some comfort and love, even if it's just in the form of food.

After appeasing my sweet tooth, I drive over to the sheriff's station. I have to let them know what Natalie said and the contradictory stories.

I also have the feeling that they might have already heard from Neil's family and the fact that I've been bothering him.

Captain Talarico is angry. He's so pissed off that if he were a cartoon character, there'd be steam coming out of his ears.

"What did I tell you?" he asks, practically slamming his hand against the desk. "You cannot bother the Gosses again. They called and they complained and now we can't talk to them about anything without their attorney."

"He's a prosecutor. Why would he need an attorney?"

"That's just how it is. He wants to protect himself. But there's no way we're getting anything out of that boy now."

This catches me by surprise and I actually take a step away from him.

"I'm sorry, I just wanted to ask Neil a question."

"Listen, I know that you're just trying to find your sister, I get that." The captain takes a deep breath. "We're doing the best that we can, but with Mr. Goss, you don't want to get on the wrong side. He may be the prosecutor, but that's his son. If we want to get any information out of that family without them clamping up, we need to be smart. We need to be able to work with them, do you understand that?"

I nod.

"This isn't the LAPD, okay? I'm sure that you have your own way of doing things. We are a small town. People know each other well. There are cliques and there are ways to get things done. This direct approach of yours, that's not going to go anywhere, and you can't intimidate them with your badge because you have no jurisdiction here."

The captain is not saying anything that I don't already know.

"Listen, I know that I messed up. I just called him and I wanted to... I thought that maybe he would tell me something."

"That kid is too smart," Captain Talarico says. "He's lying about where he was that night, and he's too smart to tell you the truth."

"How do you know that he's lying?" I ask.

"His girlfriend, Natalie, we talked to her."

"Oh, you did? I just talked to her this morning, too."

"You could have saved yourself a trip if you had just come straight here."

I nod and ask, "What did she tell you?"

"She told me that she was home all night, her brothers corroborated her story."

"You didn't confront her about what Neil told us?"

"No, we were going to hold onto that little piece of information until *you* happened to reveal it."

"I didn't tell her, but yeah, I get the point," I say, hanging my head down.

Captain Talarico narrows his eyes and puffs out his cheeks a little bit. I wait for him to go on another rampage, but he doesn't, holding himself back.

"Listen, I don't know if this Neil kid had anything to do with this, but you need to let me deal with this my way. If he was involved, then it means trouble. His father is very well-connected and he is going to do everything in his power to protect his son, trust me."

"Yes, I understand." I nod.

"Mr. Goss has big political aspirations. That's why he's here. He was a very effective and successful defense attorney for many years until he came up here and started to pretend to be an everyman. He's doing an okay job at it, but I know what he's really after."

The captain points to the chair in front of his desk and I take a seat. There are pictures of his family members in silver picture frames on his desk. I pick one up.

His wife looks like someone who enjoys crocheting and baking pies; kind, well-meaning, and without a cruel bone in her body.

"We've been together for thirty-five years," the captain says, his expression softening. "For a long time, we couldn't have children, but then we were lucky to have Alex. He's ten now."

My gaze shifts to the other picture of a little boy in Disneyland. He has a beautiful smile and the same inquisitive eyes of his father.

"You have a beautiful family."

“Thank you. I love them very much. They're my whole world,” he says after a moment.

"Most people in your position make this job their whole world."

"I've seen the movies, I've read the books, and I'm not going to make those same mistakes," Captain Talarico says. "This is a job. I work many hours. I'm going to have a good pension. I solve crimes, upkeep the peace, but these two over here, they're my number one."

"That's good," I say, nodding slightly. "That's the way it's supposed to be."

We sit in a long moment of silence, him looking at me admiring his family.

"We're forming a task force today,” Captain Talarico says. “I'm going to do everything in my power to find your sister.”

“I appreciate that.”

I walk out of his office and suddenly a wave of emotion washes over me. I clench my teeth and make a fist with my hands to try to hold it at bay.

I appreciate him not promising me anything. Cops tend to make a lot of empty promises.

I also appreciate him telling me that he'll keep looking, telling me not to give up hope. That kind of thing matters a lot, a lot more than you would think.

18

I make my way down the bland hallway, pausing briefly at the wall of photos with important people on the walls. The one that catches my attention is the one with Mr. Timothy Goss's name on the bottom.

He is embracing the sheriff and the mayor, practically holding court. I examine his thoughtful eyes, his distant stare, and the general aura of self-satisfaction, which emanates from him and all of the other men in the photograph.

"He's a big contributor to the precinct or at least he was before he became the prosecutor," Captain Talarico says, catching up to me. "Gave lots of money for various fundraisers."

Police departments aren't exactly a charitable organization in need of funding. In fact, most have a little bit too much funding and tend to funnel that money into all sorts of tactical gear, resulting in dubious consequences. I keep this to myself.

"This is why I need to tread lightly," Captain Talarico adds. "We don't know if Neil is involved in your sister's disappearance. We know that he's lying or maybe his girlfriend is, but there's no evidence pointing to the fact that either of them had anything to do with it. Of course, we need to find out *why* he's lying."

I nod, exhaling slowly. I know that what he's saying is true, but I also can't help but feel that people in this department are trying to tiptoe around someone who really shouldn't be tiptoed around.

"Mr. Goss can make things very difficult for us and we can't just go around making accusations."

"You mean like you would otherwise?"

He stays silent, biting the inside of his lip.

"That's the thing though, right? If he were some poor kid with a single mom who worked at Walmart, what would happen to him?"

Again, the captain says nothing.

"You'd bring him in. You would interview him, interrogate him, maybe lie to him about some of the evidence that you had. I know this because that's what we do, too. It's standard operating procedure."

"Listen, things aren't perfect. The world isn't perfect."

"You don't have to tell me that," I snap.

"I want to show you the pictures that we found on Violet's computer," Captain Talarico says, pivoting the conversation.

I swallow hard. Now, it's time to see them.

Downstairs, the captain introduces me to Mallory Daniels, the computer tech. After a brief amount of chitchat, she puts on gloves and opens Violet's laptop.

There's a bright pink sticker of a butterfly in one corner. It's bent and a little bit crooked and worn out.

Mallory pulls up a few files and turns the screen toward me. There are pictures of teenagers. They look about Violet's age.

I don't recognize any of them. They're in the basement of someone's house, most in various stages of undress. It looks like the pictures were taken by someone standing right in front of them.

Then the videos start. The teenagers make out and then eventually have sex. They're not fully naked, but not fully clothed either. Some shirts are removed, other skirts are just hiked up.

"Someone was standing right there in the middle of that room, making this video," Captain Talarico says.

I nod. The camera isn't fixed. You can tell by the way the camera pans, moves, and shakes that it is handheld.

Mallory goes to the next file and the next file and there are more like that.

"Do you think that Violet took these?" I ask.

"Don't know," she says.

One video is of Neil and Natalie. They're standing apart in a dark room and then slowly they come together and kiss.

They are partly clothed. He keeps his shirt on but pulls down his pants. Her bra stays on and her skirt comes up.

The video was shot in black and white. It's almost artistic in its style. There isn't the same zooming in on certain action shots. There isn't the constant angle from the perspective of the guy viewing the girl. It's more detached, distant, and it kind of looks like the voyeurism that existed in the other basement video as well.

Then just like that, right before the end, Violet appears on screen.

She waves hello but doesn't smile. Her hair is draped over her face.

She looks down and then up.

Her nails are painted black, which is something that I haven't seen before, and she's wearing way too much makeup. Her skin is pale. It's also in black and white and the shadows are, of course, exaggerated, but it's clear to me that this is indeed my sister.

"Is this all that you have? Are there more videos?"

"These are the main ones. There're a lot of still shots that you're welcome to look through, but they're basically created from these two videos."

I nod and shift my weight from one foot to another, trying to process what I have just watched.

"Why? Why did my sister make these?" I ask, thinking out loud.

"I don't know, but they're very different, aren't they?" Captain Talarico asks.

"Yes. They're not exactly like amateur porn," I agree.

"What is it about them? I can't quite put my finger on it."

"Well, there isn't a lot of that stuff that's in black and white and she kind of keeps her distance. That is, if she made that one in the basement as well. There's an observer element to it. Usually, there's a lot of zooming in on body parts and that kind of thing to create the effect of the viewer being part of the experience, but this one doesn't have anything like that."

He nods and I nod as well. Mallory leaves us alone in the room.

"Well, she clearly made the one with Neil and Natalie," I say. "That's not good."

"No, but they were also aware of themselves being filmed. I mean, they know that she's there."

"Yeah, that's true, but why? Why did she do that and why were they all filming themselves?"

"Are you really asking that?" Captain Talarico says with a smirk. "Have you seen teenagers today? They record themselves doing practically everything, so having sex? Yeah, that's kind of a memorable moment to put on film."

"I know."

I start to pace from one side of the room to the other. I look through the half-open blinds at the snowcapped pines outside.

There's a little kid and his mom riding a tricycle. He can't get the pedals quite right, so she pushes him along. He keeps getting frustrated and wanting her to help, but she keeps getting distracted by her phone.

I watch them do this dance for a little while until my thoughts slowly drift back to Violet.

"I have to ask them about this."

"No," Captain Talarico says, folding his hands across his chest. He sits down in the chair, leans back, and it makes a loud squeaking sound.

"You're not going to ask them anything about this. Both Neil and Natalie are minors and their parents are entitled to be in the room during any sort of interrogation."

This would be a problem to deal with, with a regular teenager, but given who Neil's father is this situation has to be dealt with very carefully.

"You realize, of course, that if we tell Mr. Goss about these videos and he sees them, he can press charges against your sister," the captain adds.

I bite my lower lip and nod very slowly. Yes, that idea has just dawned on me.

Making videos of underage people in intimate situations is a very serious crime. My sister was the one who was recording this content. I breathe out slowly, trying to figure out the best way to approach this.

"What are you going to do?" I ask.

"I don't know yet. We have to talk it over. We have to go through various options," he says, thinking out loud. "Obviously, according to this video, they were willingly participating in it, but who knows what happened before the tape started rolling. Does this video even have anything to do with her disappearance?"

"What about Natalie?" I ask. "What if I talk to *her* about it? What if I don't mention the video directly, but maybe ask about the possibility of it existing? I'm not sure yet."

He considers this option.

"I could talk to her after school. I can ask her again about why Neil would say that they were together that night. Maybe she can give us a clue. Perhaps there are rumors that these videos exist. I can mention that."

Captain Talarico tilts his head to one side.

"I like the idea of you coming to her as Violet's sister," he finally says, "not in the official capacity. The problem is that we don't really know if this has anything to do with anything. But maybe we can get some information without her mom getting involved."

Of course, we are skirting the ethical line. Anyone under the age of eighteen is entitled to have their parent present during our questioning. But I won't be there in any official capacity and, if I were, she probably wouldn't talk to me.

"Okay," I say, shaking my head and extending my hand. "I'll go talk to her and feel her out."

"Do not mention anything specific about this video. Push her, hint at it at the most, but she can't know that we have it."

"I agree." I nod.

"Take this with you." He grabs something off a desk. It's a small Sony recorder that's typically used for dictations.

"You know how to use this?"

I nod.

"I want to hear the gist of the conversation."

"You know that you can't use any of it in court or anything like that?" I point out.

"It doesn't matter. We just want to catch her in her lie if she is lying."

After grabbing lunch, I head back to the high school to get Natalie. I get there a little bit early because I have no idea when exactly she'll be coming out.

There's going to be a slew of people outside and I wonder if I'll be able to catch her at all.

I park in the visitors' section, get out and sit down on a bench right underneath the American flag flapping violently in the wind.

When the last bell rings, the doors open and kids start to stream out. There are buses lined up front and most beeline for their rides. A few head toward the parking lot to awaiting parents who quickly start their engines and try to beat the traffic down a blocked one-way street.

I keep scanning faces until I see Natalie walking out with a girl on each side. Dressed in sky high heels and a big puffy pink coat, Natalie looks like a Pantene commercial model with her bouncy blonde hair swaying in the glistening sunlight. She heads toward the parking lot and, after her friends bid her farewell, I seize my opportunity.

"Hi, Natalie." I wave, putting my phone in my pocket.

"Oh. Hi," she says, making a bubble with her gum. "What's up? Did you find Violet?"

"Actually, no, I haven't. I just wanted to ask you a few follow-up questions."

"Yeah, sure. My mom is picking me up soon, but I have a few minutes," she says, turning toward me.

"I wanted to ask you why you lied about not being with Neil," I say, focusing my eyes directly on hers.

"I didn't. We weren't together," she says without a flinch. "I got some pizza with my brothers and that's it."

"Earlier you said that you and your brothers weren't together that evening, but you were home."

"Did I? No. No, we were together, but at one point, I don't know exactly when, we went out and got some pizza."

"The three of you went together?"

"Yep." She chews with her mouth open, tries to make a bubble but it pops prematurely. She tries again and this time it becomes substantial, eventually reaching its breaking point and deflating unceremoniously.

"Which pizza shop was that?"

"Fresco's, the best one in town."

My heart drops and skips a beat. Fresco's is one of the most popular local hangouts. They have some of the best pizza west of New York City.

"Why didn't you tell me about this before?"

"Honestly, this morning I was kind of in a daze. I guess I just forgot."

I nod, uncertain as to whether I believe her or if she's actually as stupid as she sounds.

I try to think of a good way to transition to the video portion of my questioning, but then we reach the parking lot and her mom waves.

"I'm going to be late. C'mon!" Mrs. D'Achille yells.

Natalie throws a peace sign at me and climbs into the front seat of the Buick with three rows of seats.

19

I drive over to Fresco's in Big Bear Village. It was there when I was growing up and probably even when my parents first moved here. But I haven't been there in years. The memories are too difficult to deal with.

Mom brings it up sometimes and I know that Violet has been there a lot. A few times, we got takeout and I had to excuse myself and cry.

On the way to the shop, I drive down a winding road and sit in traffic behind a bunch of BMWs and Mercedes, clearly from down the hill.

A few of them are even driving with the chains still over their tires, even though it's in the fifties outside.

Some people honk to tell them to pull over but they just get flipped off, so I just laugh. Few people from down the hill know when you need to put them on or take them off. Generally, you only need them when it's snowing but you've got to remove them as soon as it warms up.

The closer I get to Fresco's, the harder it is for me to focus.

I don't want to go there. My whole body is resisting, and I try to think of something else.

I haven't seen my mom yet.

I've been here for almost the entire day. I have to go back to her place and help her with the press conference, which has been arranged for five o'clock.

I know that she should know about the videos on Violet's laptop, but how I can tell her that?

Violet is my little sister. There's a loyalty that sisters have when it comes to really personal stuff like that and not sharing those things with parents. If those videos have nothing to do with her disappearance, I'd be betraying her trust.

I know Mom wouldn't approve. Violet is so young and there's so much we still don't know.

Why was she there?

Why did she make them?

Nothing makes sense and I have no idea what it all means. If I tell my mom now, before I know the answers, and Violet comes back, and the videos had nothing to do with her disappearance, my mom will never look at her the same way.

I had boyfriends when I was a teenager, guys I snuck around with, made out with, kissed.

I did more than that with a few of them in the back seat of their cars.

That was before everyone needed to record absolutely every part of their life.

Today, nothing seems private and the kids growing up now record everything.

Is that all it is?

Was Violet just commemorating this event?

I don't know the answers to these questions and about a hundred others.

All I know is that I'm not ready to tell my mom anything until I know more.

I MAKE my way past small hills of black snow pushed against the sides of the parking lot. There are no tourists here. All the vehicles are at least a decade old and they haven't been washed in months.

Fresco's is a local establishment, a place that anyone who's really from here knows about and enjoys their food. Few tourists know how good it is because it's located at the back of a strip mall and doesn't have much in terms of décor or ambience.

A little bit to the side of the parking lot, next to the big oak tree, I glare at the spot where my dad and I used to park. I'm tempted to take it, but I can't make myself pull in.

I'm not ready for that.

I park clear across the lot. Getting out, I briefly glance at the decaying sign outside with the missing apostrophe and chuckle to myself.

It has been this way ever since I was a teenager and I guess they just never bothered to fix it. The front door is made of glass and covered in different promotional materials, solicitations, directions, and instructions to *not ring the doorbell* and to *use the other door.*

When I open it, it makes a loud "ding-ding" sound. There's a line of about ten people inside and no one looks up from their phones.

"I'll be right with you," a peppy teen girl with her hair in a French twist says, punching something into the cash register.

She takes everybody's orders while I wait.

I take a seat on one of the plastic chairs by the front door and look at the menu: Hawaiian pizza, Minnesota pizza, Mississippi pizza.

Hawaiian has the expected pineapple slices. I squint to read what Minnesota and Mississippi have. Cheese curds and pork belly, respectively.

Hmm. Sounds odd.

The menu's a little bit different from what I remember.

I search for my favorite item, Margherita pizza. Simple, yet fresh, and something that I always used to order.

Luckily, a few minutes later, all of the people ahead of me head toward the door and I realize that they were just one big group paying individually for their slices.

"May I help you?" the girl asks.

I wonder if it'd be rude to ask for information without ordering something and so I go with a Caesar salad. I'm not quite ready to have a slice of pizza yet.

"My name's Detective Carr and I was just wondering whether you have cameras set up inside here or in the parking lot or both."

"Yes, we do," she says. "Why?"

"How far back do they go?"

"I don't know exactly." She shakes her head.

"The eighteenth?"

"Probably, I have them all on my phone here."

"Oh? You do?"

This catches me off guard.

"I'm Casey. My father is the owner here."

She smiles.

"Nice to meet you, Casey." I shake her hand. She pulls out her phone and scrolls through.

"What time on the eighteenth?"

"Ten at night. Can you let me know if... Actually, this might be easier." I pull out my phone and show her a picture of Natalie. "Do you remember this girl and whether she was here on that night?"

"Yeah, I've seen her. I don't know if she was here. Let me see. I guess I'll start around five o'clock." She pauses the video and then starts to scroll using her finger.

"Yeah, right there. Same shiny hair, right?" She plays the video and I see Natalie and her two brothers turning around, smiling, and laughing together.

"What time was this?"

"10:05 p.m.. We were about to close, but they ordered three big pizzas, so, you know, every little bit counts."

"Okay. They didn't come in any earlier that day either?"

"No, if she came in twice, I'd remember. I was here working the whole time."

"Okay. Um, hold onto that video, please. Actually, if you could, can you send it to me?" I ask.

"Sure."

I give her my email address and she forwards the video. I wait for it to arrive before paying for my food and sitting down in one of the booths.

As I take a bite and pop a crouton into my mouth, I go over what I have so far. Natalie was not lying when she said that she came here that night with her brothers, but Neil was.

What does it mean that Neil has no alibi for when Violet had gone missing? That doesn't necessarily mean that she was with Neil.

He could be lying. It could mean anything though. It could be the reason why she's missing.

I finish my salad, wash it down with an iced tea, and get up to leave. Being in this place was a lot easier than I thought it would be.

I had avoided it for so long and yet the memories of my father and being here with him have not flooded back.

I let out a deep sigh and try not to think about it. Now it's time for me to drive back to my mom's house to fill her in on everything that has happened.

20

I arrive a little bit after four in the afternoon. She's frantic and out of control. I see the posters that she has had made up. Some of them are regular 8x10 size and two are huge.

"Why didn't you come to see me earlier? Why did you leave me to deal with all of this by myself?" she asks, annoyed.

"I was doing some investigation, Mom. Interviews."

"What are you even talking about?"

There are lines of tension on her face. Her eyes are unfocused, and her hands are out of control.

Dressed in a pair of slacks and a woodsy-colored blouse, she's done her makeup extra dark with a thick amount of foundation that is slightly the wrong color.

She looks at least a decade older than she normally does and barely resembles her old self.

"Mom, why don't you..." I don't know how exactly to put it.

I want to ask her why she looks like this but having experienced what it's like for her to ask me that on numerous occasions, I know that's not conducive to creating an open dialogue.

"Mom, you look... nice, but are you okay?" I say carefully, parsing my words.

"You look like you haven't showered in days," she snaps. "Go put some makeup on. The news people are going to be here very soon. Five o'clock, remember?"

"Mom, did you organize this *with* the police department?"

"No. I did this on my own. They are coming here and I'm going to talk about my daughter."

"I know, but usually you do it *with* the police," I say.

She glares at me, her eyebrows furrow, and she puts her hands on her hips.

"I don't care what is usually done. This is my daughter and your sister who is missing."

"You don't understand. I'm not talking about procedure," I try to explain.

I sit down at the dining room table and hope that she follows me. Sometimes, when she's this out of control, just the mere act of sitting still calms her down, but in this case, it doesn't work.

Mom stares at me and I feel like a fool for making myself comfortable in such a chaotic space.

I stand up again, take a deep breath, and count to three silently to myself.

The frantic energy that's filling the living room has to go somewhere. Our house isn't very big, and suddenly, the walls start to feel like they're closing in on top of me.

"Mom," I start again, clearing my throat. "Family members of missing people usually do these sorts of announcements and conversations with the press so that you can give your personal story and get that out there. The police and the detectives who are in charge can give all of the relevant information as well. Some details they disclose, others they don't, but it's not done this way. You can't just-"

"Don't tell me what I can't do. I'm doing this. I called *Big Bear News* and I'm doing this interview."

"So, this isn't an official press conference?"

"What are you talking about?" Mom says. "The reporter, Angela Bickerson, is the one who's coming here and I'm doing a press conference."

I nod.

I realize just how out of her element she is. I know that I should have organized this myself, but she said that she could handle it and she was so confident. I was stupid enough to believe her.

"Mom, it's not a press conference if you only do a story with one reporter. A press conference is inviting the news stations to cover it. Local news. I thought that there'd be media vans coming up here."

"I thought a press conference was when I talk to the press," she says, looking lost.

"Yes, technically, but it's more than that."

"Okay. Well, let's just talk to Angela and she can start getting the word out."

Mom walks around and grabs a paper towel to clean the already over-cleaned dining room table. I'm about to say something, but I can tell that she's in no mood to hear it.

I guess she can clean if she wants to, I say to myself and pour a glass of water.

Half an hour later, just as the sun sets over the horizon and it becomes almost pitch black inside the house, I turn on the lights, and there's a knock at the door.

A petite woman in her fifties comes in with a small bag, a recorder, and a Starbucks cup. Her thick glasses give her eyes a pretty almond shape like a cat's and Mom shows her to the dining room table.

"Can I get you something to drink or eat?" she offers.

"No, I'm good. Thank you." Angela plops her bag on the chair next to her and turns on the recorder. "I'm really sorry to hear about your daughter. Your sister. I hope that the story can bring some attention to her. Can you tell me everything that has happened? Where you were, how you discovered that she was missing, any other details?"

I let my mom lead.

Even though her voice is nervous at first, she quickly gains momentum and starts to exude confidence. Angela asks us what Violet is like and what kind of things she likes to do. Mom tells her about her art and her photography. I can't help but think back to the videos that I saw earlier today.

Suddenly, my mom breaks down. Tears, big ones, start to roll down her cheeks. I've seen her distraught before, but this is different. There's a tightness to her sadness.

She's here and present, but she's also somewhere else.

I wonder if maybe my mom is also keeping a secret from me just like I'm keeping one from her. It wouldn't be the first time.

Our family has kept a lot of secrets over the years. If there was any stability in our relationship, that was probably it.

I put my arm around her and hand her a napkin. She blows her nose and wipes her tears.

Angela tilts her head to one side, nodding sympathetically and keeps asking questions.

"Oh, one more thing," Mom says after telling Angela about the phone number for the tip line. "I'm putting out a reward. Fifty-thousand dollars for any information leading to finding her…dead or alive."

She hesitates when she says that word, *dead*, and it sends a cold shiver through my body.

Fifty-thousand dollars! Where is my mom going to get that much money?

As soon as the door closes and we watch Angela make her way down the icy steps toward her car, I turn to my mom and ask, "Where are you going to get the fifty grand?"

"I don't know."

I sigh deeply and warn, "Mom, you can't say that you're putting up reward money that you don't have."

"Why not?"

"People expect to be paid."

"I don't have to pay it right away and I'm sure that I'll come up with the money if someone finds her."

"This is not how it works. You have to put that money into an account."

"Well, I will, just as soon as I have it."

I don't know what to say or how to get through to her. I know that she's desperate.

So am I, but there are things that you do and there are things that you don't do.

"I'm going to help you come up with the money. I think I can probably scrounge together $15,000 from my credit cards, but that's it. How much do you have?" I ask.

"I don't know," she says, shaking her head. "Maybe ten, if I max everything out."

"Okay. So, we'll work with the police and we'll put the money in the account. We'll make the reward $25,000. That will be enough to get people interested if anyone knows anything."

She nods and sits down on the couch, melting into it. I go to the kitchen to pour myself some tea. When I come back out, I still see her sitting there. She hasn't moved a muscle.

"At first, I was so hopeful, nervous, and out of control, but now, there's just this dread. She's gone, Kaitlyn."

"No, don't say that." I rush over, putting my mug on the coffee table, almost dropping it off the edge. A bunch of it spills over the side, but neither of us could care less.

"I just know it," Mom says.

I hate the composure in her voice. I hate the doom in her tone.

"I felt the same way when your father-"

"Don't say it."

I grab her hands and sit on the edge of the couch, staring straight into her eyes. I want to shake her out of this feeling. I want to bring back the frantic, out-of-control Mom who is doing a million things a minute just to not think about the eventuality of what might be, but I feel it, too.

It's hard to explain, but it's like after all of that energy is spent, there's this feeling that settles over you.

Maybe something that you knew all along, like it has been in the back of your mind and now, finally, it hits you.

Still, I rage.

I fight against it.

I don't want to have even that thought in me out of fear of making it come true.

"She's gone," Mom says, staring into the distance somewhere behind me.

I shake her.

I pull on her hand, but it doesn't go away.

She doesn't even focus her eyes on mine.

"She's not gone, Mom. Look at me. She's not gone. We have to believe that we can find her."

Mom slowly moves her eyes toward mine. It takes her a bit to focus and I watch the way that her pupils expand and then contract.

"I may be wrong," she says in the same absent-minded way. "I've been wrong before, but this is how I felt when we found your dad. When I walked into this house."

Tears start to stream down my face and I find myself in the past.

My hair is in two braids, a style that I haven't worn since that night. I run over the threshold, excited about the A that I'd gotten on my Mesopotamia report and suddenly, something is different.

The TV's on, along with the radio, and Mom is just standing in the kitchen, staring while the eggs burn on the stove.

Why is she making eggs for dinner anyway?

She never does that.

I walk over to her. She doesn't respond. I turn off the radio and the television. She just stands there. I turn off the stove and take the spatula out of her hand.

"What's wrong?" I ask her, but she just stares and doesn't move.

I don't know what to do. I watch her blink once, twice, and then I head to my room.

On the way there, I have to walk past the master bedroom and she grabs me right before I get to the door.

She pulls me away and she tries to close the door, but she can't do it in time.

I look over and I see him, blood all over the bedspread. He's lying on the floor, bent in half.

I start to scream, but I can't move.

She tries to move me, but I break free and run toward my father. I grab him and I try to wake him, but he's gone.

He's cold. He has been shot in the stomach twice and there's so much blood that everything is covered in it, dark and black.

Not red at all.

Oxygenated, used, but useless, on the outside of his body.

I hold him, I grab him, and I pray for him to come back. I pray for myself to come into the house a little bit earlier, but no matter what I do, I can't turn back time.

I don't know how much time passes after that, when the paramedics or the cops or somebody in uniform pulls me away. My mom is sitting on the couch, the same couch that's here today, as these people in uniform wrap a blanket around me and tell me that everything's going to be okay.

I don't believe them.

When I look at my mom's face with the desperation and the general absent-mindedness that I see there, I know that she'll never be the same and we'll never be the same.

"This is different from Dad," I say definitively.

If I am confident enough in it, it will be true, but she doesn't respond.

She doesn't fight me and she doesn't try to convince me otherwise. She just stares into space, just like she did that day when we found him.

She does that a lot. She could've stopped me from seeing him that way, but she didn't.

That's why she was standing there burning the eggs, lost in a trance, as if she'd entered some other world from which she couldn't escape.

She's like that now, so definitive and final about Violet.

Suddenly, I hate her.

I hate her incompetence.

I hate her impotence.

I hate the fact that she just makes these decisions and proclamations and she assumes that everyone's going to go with it.

"Violet is *not* Dad," I say, grabbing her hand and forcing her to her feet. "She's *not* gone."

"I'm not saying that Violet committed suicide," Mom says quietly and another pang of anger rushes through me. "I'm just saying that I feel like she's no longer with us. You don't have to feel that way, but as a mother, I know."

"As a mother, you know *nothing*," I say, pointing my finger in her face. "I'm your daughter. You let me walk to that bedroom and you let me find him that way. How dare you? How dare you take my childhood away from me like that?"

I turn around and storm off into the back bedroom, just like I'd done millions of times before in my life.

"You were twenty!" Mom yells after me as if that was supposed to make me feel better.

There's something about being in your childhood home that makes you act like a child.

It takes you back to that world where you had no power, no control, and no life.

I walk past their bedroom again, the one that she has remodeled at least three times since his death. I don't blame her for that.

If it were me, I'd probably sell the house the first opportunity I got and move clear across the country.

What I do blame her for is *not* protecting me.

What I do blame her for is believing that he had committed suicide.

Yes, that's right.

I don't think that he did, but she does and so do the police.

There are no leads, I have no proof, and I don't know if I'll ever find out the truth.

I sit on the edge of my bed just like I did when I was a kid and I bury my head in my hands. I hate being here.

I hate being in this little house with all of its demons and all of its darkness.

I hate the fact that Violet was only two-years-old when he died, and she has no real memories of the wonderful man that he used to be.

He loved her so much. He played with her, he took care of her, he changed her diapers, and he spent every waking minute that he could with her.

I probably sound like I'm just a daughter who can't accept the fact that her father committed suicide, but it's more than that.

It's the two shots in the abdomen.

It's the fact that men who commit suicide rarely shoot themselves in the guts and the fact that, if you are shot in the stomach, it takes a very long time to die.

How long was he dying for in this room before we all came home?

Why would anyone do that to themselves, even if they did want to commit suicide?

There's a knock at the door and I see my mom in the doorway. The vacant expression on her face is gone.

She's present and connected.

She sits down on the bed with me, crosses her legs, and drapes her arm across my back. The warmth that is emanating from her wraps me up as if in a thick, plush blanket and for a moment everything feels okay again.

I want to apologize, but I can't bring myself to do it.

"I'm sorry," she says quietly, her voice not so much tense, but full of sorrow. "I'm sorry I went to that place again. I don't really have much control over it, you know that, but it's still no excuse. I'm your mother and I have to be here for real."

I nod and lean my head into her shoulder. She holds me tighter.

"I love your sister very much. You know that. I know that hope is very important and we have to keep looking for her, but... I don't know. It was just this feeling I got. This cold, vapid gust rushed through me and suddenly, I felt like I did when I found your father. Like there's nothing to be done."

I nod.

She's talking now, explaining herself, and I feel a kinship toward her. I swallow hard.

"I know that in situations like this, we can give up hope or we can carry on hoping despite all evidence to the contrary, but she hasn't been gone that long and we can't give up yet."

"At no point am I saying that we're giving up," Mom says, shaking her head. "Not at all. I'm just feeling a little lost. A little sad. A little out of control. It just swept over me like a wave."

"I'm sorry for yelling at you," I say. "I know that you feel like that and I just... That's fine, but I don't want to hear it in the future."

She looks at me and her eyes get very big.

I nod and repeat myself, "I don't want to hear it. She's my sister. I'm going to keep looking for her. I'm going to find her, no matter what, and I just can't make space for this kind of negativity in my life. Not when it comes to *her*. I have to find the answers, you know?"

"Yeah, I know." Mom nods and we hold each other for a little while.

Nothing is different, but everything has changed.

21

Later that evening, I drive back to my apartment in LA. I don't want to leave, but I have another case that I'm working on and the other detectives assigned to it can only do so much.

I don't want Captain Medvil to take me off the case and there's still so much that I have to do to figure out what happened to Courtney Reynard.

I get back home to my dusty, poorly lit apartment around eleven at night and fall dead asleep. The following morning, I wake up at six and am one of the first people in the office.

Captain Medvil calls me into his office as soon as he comes in with his Dunkin' Donuts coffee cup. He quit eating donuts earlier this year when he went on what feels like his tenth diet in five years, but this time, he's actually stuck to it and managed to lose thirty pounds.

"Courtney Reynard, where are we with that?" he asks as soon as I walk in.

"Unfortunately, I don't have much of an update. I haven't talked to her friends and I haven't found out too much more from her parents."

"I know that you're distracted with your sister. Pellegrino and Ross are working on it, so get caught up. Otherwise, I can take you off and you can do some paperwork while you're here."

"No, I really want to be of use."

He nods and I walk out of his office.

Dale Pellegrino is a big-chested kid from Iowa who was one of the only Italians in his class and who moved out west as soon as he turned eighteen. He likes to go hiking, surfing, and being as Californian as possible, but his big, ruddy cheeks and his flaxen hair betray where he's really from. I find him and Rosalie Ross, who made detective about the same time I did, sitting in the break room, nursing their big cup of coffee and watching a YouTube video.

Ross keeps her hair cut short, right below the ear, and she's a fan of Sephora. You should see her when she does all of her makeup and gets dolled up for real. The fluorescent lighting in this place does not do her justice, but she could honestly be a movie star.

She's from East LA from a family of cops. Her father, her grandfather, and her two brothers are all police officers all over southern California. It was the only thing she ever wanted to do when she was a little girl. She has no problems with confrontation, being vocal and pushy, something I occasionally struggle with.

I take a seat next to them and they catch me up. I try to apologize for not being here earlier, but they've heard about my sister and they tell me not to worry.

"So far, no fingerprints and not much physical evidence," Ross says.

I pour myself a cup of coffee, lukewarm and bland, but it feels good to have something in my hand.

While we chat, I sit across from them at the Formica table and give them my full attention.

"Had she been sexually assaulted?" I ask.

Pellegrino shakes his head and admits, "I'm surprised about that, but she hadn't."

"She was found there fully clothed, but still that is a bit of a surprise," I agree.

We don't say anything for a few moments. It's rare to see a case like this. Most of the time a thirteen-year-old girl found dead almost always has been sexually assaulted in some manner.

"We talked to her friends," Ross says. "A few of them. No leads. No suspicions, really. I doubt that it's any of the ones that we spoke to."

"What about anything on her computer?"

"Actually, yes." Pellegrino nods. "She's been talking to strangers on various social media sites. She was using a lot of fake identities."

"Really?" I ask.

"Yeah." He shakes his head and bites into his sandwich. "She was going by different names, pretending to be much older, pretending to be in college. At one point, she said she was twenty-five."

"Wow. So, what do you think that means?" I ask.

"Well, about a week earlier, she had a meeting with one of them."

"One of the people that she was talking to?"

"Yep. Twenty-four-year-old truck driver. From the looks of his page, it didn't seem like he was lying about much of what he was. They met up already and they were talking about meeting up again. That night, actually, at eight."

A shiver runs down my spine as I ask him for a clarification.

"They met up already?"

"According to the text messages, yes," Ross says. "We haven't talked to him yet. We were just about to head out to do that."

"I'd like to come."

"Of course," they say in unison.

I don't know Ross and Pellegrino very well, but they have been friends for a while. So, when we get into their vehicle to drive to see the trucker, they banter back and forth, poking fun at each other's differences, starting with what they eat for breakfast, what kind of women they like.

I sit in the back and my thoughts immediately return to my sister. She's haunting me now. I think about her day and night. I know that's not the best thing for a detective, especially one who's supposed to be investigating the case of another thirteen-year-old girl, but I can't help but be distracted.

Perhaps I should step down, and remove myself from this active investigation, but I look at the two people sitting in front of me and I think wherever

I fall short, they won't. Even if I don't take the lead on this one this time, someone is going to pick up the slack. We're going to find who did this to Courtney Reynard.

I know in the deep recesses of my mind that this is a terrible thing to think. Everyone working on this case has to give it their one hundred percent attention; otherwise, the killer will go free. But the truth is that this job is like any other.

On TV, detectives are portrayed like either degenerate drunks or superheroes, and we're a bit of both. Drinking is definitely a big problem and many have a huge superhero complex to boot.

The reality, however, is that we are just people with flaws, families, and distractions. I may not have a drinking problem, but I have a missing sister problem. My thoughts are consumed with where she is right now, much more than they are on finding the killer of that dead girl.

"You seem distracted," Ross says, turning around to face me.

I hadn't realized it, but they were talking about the Reynard case again.

I catch myself looking out the window and get embarrassed. I didn't want it to be so obvious. Of course, I thought that maybe approaching them in the break room, catching up on the case, and being more involved would fool them, but they are two detectives after all.

"Listen, we're taking the lead on this," Pellegrino says, "and we'll cover for you. It's not a problem. So, if you can't be here right now, it's totally fine."

It would probably be easier if I *weren't* here. They are partners, friends, and they know how to do the interview dance together.

One is the good cop. The other is a bad cop. So, what am I exactly? The third wheel?

"No, I like to participate. I'm on this case and there's nothing more that I can do right now for Violet."

I use her name because I don't want to call her my missing sister. I don't want to give her that adjective.

"Are the cops letting you in on it?" Ross asks. "Or is it the usual small-town politics?"

"They're actually being very nice about it. I interviewed a number of her friends, got a few leads, but nothing substantial. There's one guy, the most popular kid at school, the jock, the future asshole of America. He kind of looks suspicious and his alibi is shaky. He said that he was with his girlfriend, but she said that he wasn't. Anyway, he seems to be lying. Probably is. I just have no idea if he had anything to do with Violet's disappearance."

"How long has it been?" Ross asks.

"Two days," I say. "My mom is organizing a press conference. I just hope that we can get enough news stations to show up, or any at all. This is Big Bear after all."

"What does Violet look like?" Ross asks.

I show her a picture.

She nods approvingly.

It's a terrible thing to say, but the truth is that pretty girls get looked for a lot more than less attractive ones. Not by cops necessarily, but by the media.

When was the last time you saw a girl in the news who was missing, who wasn't that perfect fit for the standard American beauty; white, blonde hair, big eyes, with the occasional breathtaking brunette thrown in?

It's one of the reasons why there are so few cases of teenage boys that get picked up by the mainstream news. People assume that they're runaways. It's hard to get the reporters to report on them, but the truth is that they go missing at approximately the same rates as teenage girls.

A FEW MINUTES LATER, we get to Jesse Broward's house. It's a small, dilapidated apartment or cottage, if you can even call it that, in the back of a four-plex. It actually resembles something like a shed that has been converted into very modest living quarters. The paint is peeling and the walls look like they're made out of paper. Out front, there's a red Camaro, waxed, cleaned, and practically licked to perfection.

Pellegrino knocks on the door while I stand behind on the walkway leading up to the porch. There isn't enough space for all of us up there. It's basically a five-by-five square with a rusting railing, which could fall over with one dirty look.

"Jesse, come out," Pellegrino says in his booming voice.

About ten knocks later, the door creaks open and a man with an extreme hangover answers. His hair is long and falling shabbily in his face. His skin is so white it practically looks see-through. I can smell last night's beer on his breath when he coughs without covering his mouth.

"What are you doing here?" he demands to know.

"I told you we would be stopping by," Pellegrino says, surprising me.

It's not normal police procedure to notify people of us showing up. They tend to clam up when you do that or call lawyers.

"No, you didn't," Jesse says. "Who are you?"

We all flash our badges and Pellegrino asks if we can come in.

We can only enter with a warrant or an invitation, and luckily Jesse offers the latter.

Walking into the studio apartment, I see a mattress lying on the floor in the corner. The bed is unmade and there's no bottom sheet or even a pillow.

"Is this your permanent address?" Pellegrino asks.

"Yeah. So what?" He plops into an expensive gaming chair in front of an enormous, curved computer screen.

There's nowhere else to sit and we wouldn't sit anyway. I stand in the doorway, looking around, taking it all in. The only window is a single pane and heat is streaming in through it. It's covered up by two short black curtains, just long enough to cover the glass. Instead of a curtain rod, the curtains are held up by pins and one looks like it's about to let go.

"Yeah, I live here," Jesse says.

"For how long?"

"I don't know. Couple months. Why?"

"Have you been in contact with a girl by the name of Courtney Reynard?"

"No."

"Does she look familiar now?" Pellegrino pulls out his phone and shows him a picture of her.

"That's Mary-Anne."

"Mary-Anne?" Pellegrino laughs. "Who the hell is named Mary-Anne anymore?"

"I don't know. She is. Why does it matter?"

"Well, it matters because this girl's real name is Courtney Reynard, and she was found hanging from a tree."

"What? What are you talking about?" He gasps and stands up.

This is the moment.

This is what we look for, the reaction.

A person who has committed a murder reacts in a very different way from a person who is pretending to have never heard of this girl.

I'm thrown off a bit by Pellegrino's approach. Usually, the way to do this is to ask a few questions, see if the suspect trips up and refers to the victim in past tense. How would he know that she was no longer with us if he wasn't the one that took her out? That sort of thing.

But in this case, I think Pellegrino played it right.

Jesse looks genuinely surprised, taken aback, and shocked by the fact that Courtney's dead.

"No. You guys are shitting me, right? Mary-Anne is not dead."

"Yep. D-E-A-D," Pellegrino spells it out for him. "Now, why don't you tell us what you know about that?"

"I don't know anything. Apparently, I don't even know her real name."

He shifts his weight nervously from foot to foot, but not in a guilty sort of way, more like he is surprised and uncertain as to what to do next.

"When was the last time you saw her?" Ross asks.

"The one and only time I saw her was about a week ago." Jesse grabs his phone.

"You're not going to be deleting any texts there, are you?" Pellegrino asks, looking over his shoulder.

"No, I'm trying to show you something."

Jesse shows him the text string as Pellegrino shines his flashlight on the screen.

"We met up last Tuesday. She didn't look anything like her pictures. I mean, they were filtered or something. Who the hell knows? She was too young. I knew that she was underage and nothing happened."

"What do you mean?"

"We met at a coffee shop. Starbucks, right on Melrose. She kept telling me that she was twenty-one, but I could tell that there was no way she was that old. I didn't want to talk to her after that."

"Oh, yeah, because you're such an honorable guy?" Ross asks.

"Listen, I was looking for a date, a girl that I could, you know, hang out with, have a good time with. I'm not into kids and she was just looking to fuck around."

"What do you mean by that?" Ross asks.

"I don't know. She just gave me this vibe. It's hard to explain. It's like she was having a good time just by lying and seeing me react to her lies. It was so stupid. I mean, it was so obvious. She just wanted to catch me or something."

"So, what happened then?" I ask.

"I bought one cup of coffee. I talked to her maybe for ten minutes, standing up at the counter. We didn't even sit down. Then I asked her why the hell she lied to me."

"And?" I ask. "Did she tell you?"

"She said that she wasn't lying. She said that she was twenty-one and the girl in the picture. She said that I was the one that was wrong."

"She kept telling you that her name was Mary-Anne?" I ask.

"Yeah, like I'm some sort of idiot. I mean, her name might have been Mary-Anne, but at that point, I already didn't believe a word coming out of her mouth. I wasn't sure if it was a set-up or what the hell was happening."

He gasps for air, running over his words.

"That was it. I left," Jesse says after a brief pause. "You can go talk to the employees there or get the tape or whatever, but you'll see that that was it and when she texted me after that, I didn't text her back. I blocked her, actually, because she wouldn't stop."

A part of me is skeptical. I'm tempted to not believe him.

Ross, Pellegrino, and I exchange looks all asking the same question. If this guy is telling us the truth, then what could have happened?

"What about on the eighteenth?" I say. "I saw in your messages that you had plans to meet up."

"No. Absolutely not." He shakes his head.

I open her Instagram account and I show him what I'm looking at: messages from him to her to meet up that night.

"I did not write them. Are you serious? This is not... No. Absolutely not." He looks at the screen again. "No. I told her that I would never meet with her again. She was psycho. I mean, she was like a little kid, but she was insane. I did not write those messages."

"So, why are they here?" I ask, staying calm.

Suddenly, the room starts to feel incredibly small and is shrinking more with every second.

We walk out of the apartment and don't say a word until we get to the vehicle.

"What do you think?" Pellegrino asks, turning toward us as we form a huddle.

"I got the feeling that he's telling us the truth," I say. "He seemed genuinely shocked that she's dead, but they had plans to meet up that night, right? I mean, that's what the text messages say."

"I agree, except for that one bit. I mean, do you think that he would have met up with her again?" Pellegrino asks Ross.

Ross shakes her head.

"That guy seemed genuinely freaked out. I don't know. I've never seen that kind of reaction before. He was so put off. He wasn't pretending like he didn't know her. He was kind of angry about who she said she was, but to meet her again? I don't know. Is there any way to check whether the messages are fake or not?"

"There's a way to find out *when* they were sent, but how could she have faked them?" I ask.

When we return to the station, I go over to talk to Ben Lawrence, the computer tech and show him what we have. He squeezes me in and thinks about it for a moment.

"There's no way that she had his log-in info?"

"I don't know," I say. "I mean, of course that would be the easiest way, right? She'd log in, she'd pretend that they had plans to meet up, but to what end? I mean, why?"

"I don't know," Ben says, shaking his head.

He wears a button-down shirt and his hair is cut short. No glasses, though, so not exactly a full cliché of what a person in his job would look like, but pretty close.

Ben is friendly, gregarious, and actually seems to like women more than computers. Plus, he's good at what he does. We trust him.

"I'll go through the files again. I'll see if she logged into any other devices to try to trace this back. Give me a few hours."

I nod and leave him to it.

22

I go back to my desk and try to figure out what else could have happened. I mean, the simplest explanation is, of course, that Jesse is lying. He did have plans to meet with her.

I go over everything that I have seen of him in that conversation; the room, the facial expressions, the anger. He was quite angry.

Angry people are capable of a lot and if he were that angry when he was talking to us, detectives from the LAPD, total strangers, then how angry would he have been with a girl who dared to lie to him?

Unfortunately, in this business, girls tend to be killed for a lot less than that. A man's anger goes a long way and casts long shadows.

I decide to go get something to eat from the vending machine just as I start to feel the lump in my throat. When you do this for a while, you tend to try to forget that these are people's lives that you're dealing with. These aren't just stories.

These aren't just things that happen to other people. These are their whole lives, and you come into contact with them at the worst possible points.

You get to tell the story of their deaths.

You get to find out what happened.

You get to give people closure, their families mostly.

We talk about justice being served, but is it really ever served? The people who are dead are still dead. There's no bringing them back. Their killers are put in prison. Some are executed. That doesn't change the outcome though. That doesn't take away the pain of that night. It doesn't bring back anything that happened. So, justice, vengeance, or whatever you want to call it, that's just for the surviving family members. That's what they get. What does the victim get?

LESS THAN AN HOUR LATER, Ben Lawrence walks up to my desk with a big grin on his face like he has found something.

"What's up?" I ask, popping a pretzel into my mouth.

"Somebody logged into Jesse Broward's Instagram from Courtney's computer and texted him."

"Really?" I ask. "How do you know?"

"I didn't check for this earlier but when I went through it again, I saw that somebody had logged into his Instagram at precisely 6:50 p.m."

"Courtney?" I ask.

"They texted back and forth and set up a meeting. Instagram was open on the Chrome browser and it was logged into his account. Her Instagram was open on Safari."

"What does that mean?" I ask.

"Someone using her computer was able to talk back and forth and set this whole thing up to make it look like they had met up that night or had plans to meet up that night."

"Courtney?" I ask again.

"Either Courtney or someone using her computer pretending to be Courtney."

"Oh, wow. Huh," I say out loud, furrowing my brow.

"What could this mean?" Ben asks.

"Well, do you think that she did it?"

"She might have done it. But it might have been someone else using her computer," he offers.

That seems unlikely, I say to myself.

When we walk over to Ross and Pellegrino to share the news, they seem as perplexed as I am.

"Who else was in the house at that time?" Ross asks rhetorically.

"Her parents," I offer.

"But they wouldn't have done anything like that, right?" Pellegrino asks.

We shake our heads. It seems unlikely.

"Well, the only thing I know," Ben says, "is that it was someone using her computer and according to the GPS, the computer was at her house. So, it could have been her. It could have been her parents, or I guess some other person who came over to the house and did this."

"It was definitely not Jesse texting her back, right?" I confirm.

"Definitely not. The messages look like they had been read almost immediately and they were read from right there in that house, which couldn't have been the case since he wasn't there."

I nod as the wheels start to turn in my mind about all of the possibilities. There's still a lot to confirm, especially when it comes to all of this technology stuff, but for now, we all know what we need to do. We need to talk to the parents.

I reach out to Mrs. Reynard while Pellegrino calls Dr. Reynard. We try to organize a time for them to come in. Mrs. Reynard seems distracted and a little bit annoyed when I call, which is an unusual reaction from someone who should be consumed entirely by the death of her daughter. Again, it's hard to judge in these situations. They had just had the funeral and her husband had gone back to work, leaving her alone in the house.

She says that she absolutely cannot come tonight, and I offer to stop by.

I wait for her to say no, but she doesn't.

When Pellegrino gets off the phone with Dr. Reynard, he says that he couldn't even get through.

"They told me that he was in surgery. Apparently, some sort of big emergency thing."

"I can't believe that he went there the night of his daughter's funeral," Ross says, shaking her head.

She'd recently adopted a little squeak of a dog and has spent a small fortune on his bed, clothes, and everything else that people who love dogs more than people usually do. When she brought him over to the precinct my heart melted and I immediately wanted to get one, too. But unlike Ross, I live alone and the long hours I put in at work would just be too unfair to an animal.

"I find that hard to believe as well, except that we should all know what it's like to be a workaholic," I point out. "Sometimes it's easier just to spend your time working, distracting yourself rather than really feeling the moment, the pain of it all."

Our eyes meet and Ross and Pellegrino are the first ones to look away. I know that they know what I mean. Everyone here does.

We all like to work a lot. The hours busy our minds and help us forget whatever unhappiness we deal with on a daily basis in our personal lives.

That is the not-so-secret secret about detectives. We're all running away from something, pretending that something's not happening.

We like to stay busy. We like to stay active. We like to log lots of hours so that we don't have to think about life and the meaninglessness of it all too much. We each seek solace in whatever is available and appealing; religion, philosophy, alcohol, toxic relationships.

For many years, that's exactly how I dealt with my father's death. I don't believe that he committed suicide for a moment, but Mom does and we have basically reached an understanding of letting each other believe what we wish.

We're like those families on opposite ends of the political spectrum. If we want to be happy and continue to celebrate holidays together and have some semblance of a family, we have to agree to disagree and never talk about certain things.

"I don't know many doctors," I say, "but I have a feeling that they're workaholics just like cops and maybe this is the only thing that he could think to do to take his mind off things."

They nod. They know I'm right. I'm not trying to take his side and it's a totally crappy thing to do to your wife, who doesn't have the luxury of escape, but sometimes it's the only thing you can do to protect yourself.

"Why don't I drive over to Mrs. Reynard's?" I say. "I will talk to her and then reach out and let you know if it's anything of interest."

They nod. Their shift is ending. They've been working on this non-stop, logging a lot more hours than I have.

"We can always interview Dr. Reynard tomorrow morning or maybe I can even go talk to him tonight. We'll see how long it all takes."

"We can wait to do both tomorrow morning," Pellegrino suggests.

“No.” I shake my head. "I want to get this done. I think I'm going to try to get the press conference organized for my sister tomorrow morning and it's about a three-hour drive out there."

“The mountains are going to get a lot of snow," Ross says. “It's going to drop into the fifties here. Lots of rain is expected.”

"Yeah? Then it’s going to be in the thirties up there," I say with a nod. "Let me talk to Mrs. Reynard just in case I get snowed in. Then we can go from there. I'll call you."

I arrive at Mrs. Reynard's Brentwood home just as the sprinklers come on. She has a big, wide, open lawn and a Tudor-style home that, from the looks of it, is probably more than 5,000 square feet. The façade is white with neat trim around the windows. The front is immaculately landscaped, and I doubt that she does any of it herself.

I park my car right up front and make my way up the driveway. I see her through the kitchen window, talking on the phone. She walks back and forth nervously and gestures wildly. Her hair is pinned up on top of her head and it looks like she's even wearing glasses, something I haven't seen before.

The door knocker is elegant and thick, and it makes a loud dinging sound. I use it instead of the doorbell. I stand on a welcome mat that says, *Welcome to Our Home* in elaborate script.

As soon as she opens the door, I smell the irresistible scent of cinnamon streaming in from the kitchen. My mouth starts to water. It immediately reminds me of the cinnamon cookies that my mom used to make every fall.

"Mrs. Reynard, I'm sorry to bother you again."

She sees me and the expression on her face shifts. It's almost like she takes a breath of fresh air. It's hard to explain. The tension seems to vanish, which is an unusual thing to happen.

"I have to go," she says into the phone and waves me inside.

The foyer of the house is grand and beautiful. There's an enormous bouquet of flowers on the table right out front and the crystal chandelier sparkles in the night light.

"Can I get you something to drink or eat? I'm just about to have some of the food that people brought over for the funeral. If you want any, there's plenty."

I'm about to say no, but I nod before I can. I follow her into the pristine marble kitchen with Shaker-style cabinets and brushed brass doorknobs. The farmhouse sink is empty of dishes and even patted dry. It has either never been used or has been immaculately cleaned.

There are two islands parallel to one another. The one without the sink is covered in food platters and the rest of the kitchen, the entire perimeter, is covered in white flowers.

"We just had the funeral today," she says, and I give her a nod.

She's still dressed in her black clothes; black jacket, black pencil skirt, and black blouse underneath, but she's no longer wearing her heels or pantyhose. Her feet are bare and the nail polish on her fingernails is peeling, like she had been picking at it.

"Can I make you some tea?" she asks. "I'm going to have some myself."

"Yes, that actually sounds great." I nod and take a seat at the circular marble table across from the second island.

The chairs are plush and gray with gold legs. I've never sat on a kitchen chair that was this comfortable.

She brings over two mugs. Hers says, *Happy Fall, Y'all* and mine says, *Hang in there*. I doubt that she got these on purpose, but mine is particularly poignant in this situation.

She holds open a box of tea bags, each one organized in its own particular container, and I grab the orange crush one, herbal, caffeine-free. I plop it into my mug of hot water as she offers me sugar in a silver sugar bowl.

"No, thank you." I shake my head.

She doesn't take any for herself but tosses two bags of chamomile into her mug. She sits across from me and we don't say anything for a few moments.

I wonder where all of her friends are and why they're not here or maybe her family. If anyone were here, I wouldn't be able to talk to her like this, but this is my in. This is my opportunity.

"I wanted to ask you about your daughter," I say, taking a sip of my tea and letting the warm liquid run down my throat.

23

Mrs. Reynard sits across from me. She looks tired and worn out. I know that she has been through a lot, but I need her help.

"Sure," she says with a shrug. "What do you want to know?"

I reach into my purse. This is the moment of truth.

"I'm going to record your answers. Is that okay?" I say, pulling out a recorder.

At this point, many people usually tell me to get out of their house and call their lawyer. It's illegal to record confidential conversations, including private conversations or telephone calls without a two-party consent in California. It's actually a crime to record a private conversation, but someone can legally record a communication made in a public place. The law also doesn't apply to police and some private citizens when recording a conversation to gather evidence of an offense.

She looks at the recorder and nods gently.

"I just want to make sure that I get everything right," I say, looking at the recorder again.

"Yeah, whatever. It's fine," Mrs. Reynard says, rather despondent.

I turn it on and I start asking her about her daughter.

"Can you tell me what Courtney was like, growing up?"

Mrs. Reynard takes a deep breath and exhales very slowly.

"She's been a very difficult child ever since her brother was born."

Mrs. Reynard averts her eyes and doesn't meet mine but talks as if she's talking to no one in particular.

"We didn't mention this earlier, but she was diagnosed with borderline personality disorder."

"What does that mean?"

"It's difficult to explain, but it's a mental illness with a distorted sense of self and strong emotional reactions. She has a hard time with relationships, and she often struggles with feelings of emptiness, abandonment, and general detachment from reality."

Mrs. Reynard rattles off the description as if it's a text she had memorized.

"So, what was it like to have her live here? What was *she* like?" I say, prodding for more details.

"Courtney lies all the time," Mrs. Reynard says, shifting back and forth between past and present tense. It's almost as if she isn't fully accepting the fact that her daughter is dead. "She stole her grandmother's credit cards and her identity."

"She did?"

"Yep." She nods. "She bought a house."

"What do you mean?"

"It's ridiculous. She bought one of those dilapidated houses for $50,000 in Kentucky. The ones that they have on those websites, *Cheap Old Houses* or something like that. The whole thing is just a mess. She bought it with her grandmother's money and registered it under her name. Now, we owe all these taxes, and I don't even know if we can even sell that house again."

Wow, I say to myself.

"She stole my identity as well, or rather, my credit cards. We had to keep all of our private information locked up. She bought clothes, jewelry, whatever. She didn't even care that we would find out when the statement came. She pretended to be other people online."

"Okay. Tell me more about that." I want to ask her why she hadn't told me any of this before, but it doesn't feel like the right time. So, I bite my tongue.

"She's uncontrollable," Mrs. Reynard says.

Again, present tense. Why? Why does she keep lapsing into this? She was just at her daughter's funeral and now it seems like she doesn't believe she's dead.

"My daughter is totally uncontrollable," Mrs. Reynard says.

A tear runs down her cheek.

She doesn't say anything for a moment, and I don't ask any questions. We sit here in silence, but then it gets to be too long. I prod her again.

"What did you do when you found out?"

"About what?" she asks.

"About the house, the credit card theft, the purchases, the identity theft, all of it."

"We talked to her about it. We fought about it. She promised not to do it again and then she did. We had to hide everything in our house like we were living with a thief. Do you know what that's like?"

Mrs. Reynard looks up into my eyes and glares.

"I can't even imagine," I say. "What about the people that she talked to online? Have you caught her talking to these men?"

"I banned her from using the computer. I took it away and she bought another one. She had her phone. I took that away. She used her iPod. How the hell do you even use an iPod to go online? I have no idea. She didn't listen to anything we said. We made threats. I was going to call the cops, but my husband stopped me. He didn't want her to have a record, even one for a juvenile. We just couldn't do anything to control her."

She takes a sip of her tea and then looks straight into my eyes again.

"I caught her using all of these fake identities, pretending to be in her twenties while she was on these dating sites. It was ridiculous. Some thirteen year olds can possibly pass for being eighteen, but not Courtney. She looks like a child. When she put on makeup and got dressed up, she looks even younger."

I wait for her to continue.

"Looked even younger," Mrs. Reynard corrects herself. "I'm sorry I keep doing that."

"Did she use her real pictures online?" I ask, after shifting my weight in the seat.

“I don’t know. Probably not when she was talking to strangers. She would just meet up with these guys as this fake person and when they would ask her about why she looks different, she would just say that she doesn't. I mean, how does that work?"

I take a deep breath and exhale, trying to collect my thoughts.

"That was a very dangerous thing that she was doing,” I finally say.

"Yeah, I know."

“Did she know you knew?"

“No… Well, sort of," Mrs. Reynard says. "She left her computer out a few times, logged in. I read the messages. She always used Facebook because older people are on Facebook. She was never on TikTok where you'd find all the people her own age. It's like she wanted this to happen."

"You don't mean that," I say.

The words escape my mouth before I can stop them. I realize that they are steeped in judgement and it's the last thing that she probably wants to hear, but she doesn't say anything and barely reacts. "What happened that night?"

"Nothing. I was home, just like I said."

"You didn't use her computer, not even to check on her?"

"No. Not that night. I went upstairs, I went to bed and took an Ambien. I haven't been sleeping well for years. I take them almost every night and I know it's not good, but I just need to rest."

I swallow hard.

"Why would Courtney pretend to meet up with Jesse again?" I say, tilting my head.

I have to play this just right. I have to add just the right amount of pressure or I'm going to blow it. If I push her too hard and she's not ready to say it (whatever *it* is), she can clam up and I'll have little to go on.

"She did? You know who Jesse is?"

"Yes. I saw the messages. I saw that they had met and that she kept messaging him after that. He didn't want anything to do with her, huh?

"Well, someone had logged into his account and pretended that they were still talking. Someone did it from your house."

Her face drops. Before she says anything else, Dr. Reynard walks into the kitchen.

I jump, but I catch myself and plaster a casual smile while waving hello. I cover the recorder with my hand and quietly slide it into my pocket without turning it off.

"Were you on Courtney's computer that night?" Mrs. Reynard asks her husband.

"What night?"

"*That* night. The *night* that she disappeared."

"No," he says. Standing in the doorway with his shoulders broad, he shakes his head.

"Yes, you were," Mrs. Reynard says. "I remember she had the laptop down here. You opened it and you looked at it."

He walks past her to the fridge.

She continues anyway with, "Did you see the message from Jesse?"

"Who's Jesse?"

"You know who Jesse is. He's that guy, that trucker that she met up with who turned her away."

"I have no idea what you're talking about, but I think it's time for Detective Carr to leave. We need to have some time to grieve."

"You need some time to grieve? Really? Don't make me laugh," Mrs. Reynard snaps. "You could barely wait until her funeral was over to go back to the hospital."

"I had an emergency, Maureen, you know that."

"Someone could have covered for you; I know that much. You didn't want to be here. You didn't want to deal with this…with her death."

"Yeah. So, what? Work's how I deal with everything, you know that."

"What about me? What about me needing my husband after my daughter was brutally murdered?" She gasps for air as she says that.

"Listen, Detective Carr, I think we all need to just relax a little bit and we can talk to you about this some other time," Dr. Reynard says in a cold, detached tone of voice.

"Why did you write that message from Jesse? How did you even log into her computer?" Mrs. Reynard continues.

"I did no such thing, and you know it," he snaps. "Courtney snuck out and someone grabbed her. Some sick person did this to her. He watched her suffocate and die. Detective Carr and the LAPD have to figure out who did it. Not us."

A shiver runs down my spine, followed by another that runs down the back of my neck, followed by another. How could he know that? How could he know that she had suffocated and that the guy who hung her watched her die?

Dr. Reynard approaches me and takes a step away to usher me through the door, but I don't move.

"How did you know that?" I ask. "How did you know that Courtney didn't die quickly?"

"What do you mean?"

"That was never revealed to anyone. She was found hanging, but no one told you or anyone else that she had suffocated and that she wasn't dead when she was hung there."

"Wait a second." Mrs. Reynard gets up from her chair. "You weren't here that night."

"Be quiet," he says.

"You weren't here when I went to bed. When I woke up, I looked over where you were supposed to be, but you weren't there. Bill, where were you?"

"I was right there with you. I don't know what you want me to say. You really think I, what, killed Courtney? C'mon."

Mrs. Reynard's eyes widen as she stares at her husband in disbelief.

"You weren't here that night," she whispers, shaking her head.

My stomach ties in knots and I take a few steps toward him, reaching for my weapon.

This is it. I'm going to arrest him.

Just as I start to pull it out of the holster, Dr. Reynard turns and points a 9mm at me.

"Tim, what are you doing?" Mrs. Reynard gasps, placing her hand over her mouth. Her already pale face turns practically green as all the blood drains away.

"You get away from me," he snaps at her.

I take a small step away and then another.

"Not you."

He grabs my hand and pulls me close. He places the gun to my temple and I can feel my heartbeat against the smoothness of the steel.

"You think you can just come in here and accuse me of these things?"

I take a few forceful deep breaths as he presses the weapon harder against my head.

No matter what happens, I have to stay calm.

I still have two aces up my sleeve; he doesn't know that I have a weapon and he doesn't know that all of this is being recorded.

24

"Dr. Reynard, please put the gun down," I say as calmly as possible.

I feel my heart pumping, practically jumping out of my chest. My heart is beating so hard that I can barely hear or think as the blood rushes around in my head. "Dr. Reynard, please put the gun down."

"No," he utters through his clenched teeth.

"Tim, do as she says. What are you doing?" Mrs. Reynard yells.

"Maureen, shut the hell up. This doesn't concern you."

"It doesn't concern me? You have a gun pointed at the detective's head."

I swallow hard. I hate to say this, but she's making it worse. The energy in the room is amplifying.

Then someone says, "Mom? Dad?" It's a tiny little voice belonging to their five-year-old.

He's dressed in pajamas, with little trucks and monkeys on them. The pants and shirt are mismatched, like they belong to two different sets.

His hair is tousled and he looks like he's been sleeping.

"Dennis." Mrs. Reynard runs over and wraps her son up in her arms.

"Take him upstairs," Dr. Reynard commands.

"No," she whimpers.

I hold my breath. I pulse my fingers inside my palm nervously shifting my weight from one foot to another. The barrel of the gun is still pressed tightly to my temple.

"We're staying here until you let her go." Her voice is quiet but filled with resolve.

"I'm not letting her go, Maureen!" Dr. Reynard yells, his eyes are bloodshot.

His forehead is covered in sweat and there are big underarm stains on his button-down shirt stretching down his back and up his front.

I don't know what to do.

If it were just the two of us, I could reach for my weapon and try to shoot him, but it's a close call.

He's pressing his weapon right to my temple. If I hesitate, if I don't get it right, I'm dead.

"You haven't done anything wrong yet, Dr. Reynard. You can still let me go and we can just talk about this."

This isn't true, of course, but I have to try something.

"People know I'm here, but no one suspects this to be anything but a general interview," I add, careful not to make it a threat.

"You can't believe that," Dr. Reynard says, pushing the gun further into my skin. "Go sit down."

I do as he says. I take a seat in the chair where I'd sat behind the marble table in the kitchen.

Dennis, their son, starts to cry.

"I don't want to play cops and robbers now," Dennis mumbles through the tears. "Make Daddy stop."

Mrs. Reynard tries to calm him down, but it's to no avail.

"You've done nothing wrong," I repeat myself. "You can take all of this back."

"No, I can't," he says, shaking his head.

"Tell me what happened," I say, knowing that the recording is still going.

"She just wouldn't stop. She wouldn't stop, Maureen!" He turns around and yells in the direction of his wife. "Courtney would just lie and lie."

"I know about the house," I say, pivoting the conversation.

"The house was the least of it. It cost fifty grand for some old, dilapidated plantation in Kentucky. Five acres, 2,000 square feet, not a single straight piece of wood in the place, but who cares?"

"So, that wasn't a big deal?" I ask.

"It was, but it wasn't the stupidest thing she did."

He gestures wildly with the gun as he talks. I see a moment here and there where I could reach for my weapon and shoot him, but then I glance over at his son.

He'll remember this.

If I kill his father right in front of him, he will never be okay.

"Take Dennis away!" Dr. Reynard yells and my blood runs cold.

"No," Mrs. Reynard snaps back.

She holds him tighter. She's still in the doorway and I want to ask her to leave, but I'm afraid of what will happen if she does.

"Courtney wouldn't stop lying. She just got such satisfaction out of it. Do you know what she did besides the house?"

"What?" I ask.

"She went to my work and took one of my lab coats. You know, the one with my name on it? She saw my fucking patients. She actually walked up to the emergency room and she had the audacity to take them in the back, ask them about their medical histories, ask them what was wrong, and then treat them."

His eyes flicker wildly as the anger brewing inside of him reaches a boiling point.

"I'm really sorry," I say quietly.

But what I really want to ask is why.

What I really want to tell him is that maybe she was just trying to be like him, to emulate him. But I worry that will just make him angrier.

"How dare *she* pretend to be me?" Dr. Reynard demands to know, using the gun as if it were a pointer in a lecture hall.

I look closer to see how tightly he's holding it in his hand and debate as to whether or not I should shoot him next time he pulls it away from me.

If I do as I was trained, I'd have to aim center mass, right in the heart and he'd die right before us.

But what happens if I shoot him in the arm or the leg?

What will happen to that gun?

How good is he with it?

What if he knows how to use it?

What if he shoots his wife, his child, or *me*?

"What happened at the hospital?" I ask, trying to calm him down, but it has the opposite effect.

"My daughter pretended to be me. I found out about it that night!" he roars. "Did you know that she did that, Maureen? That she embarrassed me like that? She went to my work and she actually *prescribed* people medication. She could have killed someone. I could have lost my license. My boss called me into his office. You know how much I hate that son of a bitch? His cockiness, his self-importance? Do you know what it was like for *me* to sit there and to listen to that lecture like I was a little child? No one had talked to me that way for years. Not since my father…"

"What are you trying to tell me, Tim?" Mrs. Reynard asks, standing up.

She pulls away from her son and puts her hand over her face to cover up something that just occurred to her.

Dr. Reynard and I exchange glances.

I already know the answer; what I don't have is proof.

"What did you *do*, Tim?" She runs over and throws her fists at his chest. "Tell me what you did."

"Nothing. Nothing that wasn't absolutely necessary, Maureen, and you know it. It was ... Nothing. I didn't do anything." He flip-flops back and forth, dodging the question.

Mrs. Reynard looks into her husband's eyes with a wild look of disbelief.

"You killed her?" She asks, gasping for air.

"It was an accident," he says, tears streaming down his face. "It was... It was an accident. I didn't mean for it to happen."

"What did you *do*?" She hits him with her fists, shaking his shoulders.

"She impersonated me, Maureen. She didn't have the right to do that."

"What did you do?" she whispers, tears streaming down her face.

"I went up to her room to talk to her. I didn't tell you because I didn't know *how* to tell you. I didn't want you to worry. I just wanted to handle it."

"What did she do? What did she say?" Mrs. Reynard pleads.

"She just ... She lied about it at first. She denied ever even being there. When I kept pushing her, she told me to fuck off. She told me that it was none of my business. She told me that she could do whatever the hell she wanted to. She was completely out of control and I couldn't handle it anymore. I just grabbed her. It was just an accident."

"What? What was an accident?" She pushes, looking deep into his eyes.

I glance down at the gun in his hand. It's still tucked into his palm. His fingers are wrapped tightly around it. It's almost as if it has somehow become an extension of his hand. He's big, tall, and isn't a stranger at the gym. There's no way I can overpower him.

There's Mrs. Reynard to think about. What would she do if I attacked her husband? I could shoot him, of course, but Dennis is standing in the doorway, pressed against one side of the wall. His eyes, which are as big as saucers, have a lost, far away expression in them. He looks confused and on the verge of tears.

I want to ask him to go upstairs, but I don't want to remind his parents that I'm still here.

"It was an accident," Dr. Reynard says.

He's grabbing onto his wife, pulling her into his arms, and has his head buried in her shoulder. This was how I remember seeing them the first time at the precinct. Heads pointed toward each other, grasping onto one another.

"I wanted her to admit the truth. I needed to hear it from her own mouth."

"What? That she was lying?" Mrs. Reynard whimpers.

"Yes! I mean, she would just go and meet up with all of those guys and tell them the truth, admit all of her lies to them. Why couldn't she do that with me?"

"What did you do?" Mrs. Reynard says, wiping her eyes.

Her skin looks sallow, and her eyes have big black rings at the bottom from smeared mascara.

"We had an argument. I yelled at her. I begged her to tell me the truth. I even cried, broke down, but she wouldn't do it. Why not? Why wouldn't she do it?"

"She's Courtney and she's as stubborn as her father," Mrs. Reynard says quietly.

"I just lost control, Maureen. I just grabbed her, wrapped my hands around her neck, and held her for too long. I thought that I would just make her feel the anger that I felt. I just wanted to hurt her, but not *hurt* her. Do you know what I mean? Then she just passed out and it was too late."

"Too late for what?" Mrs. Reynard whispers.

"She was dead."

"She was dead?" Mrs. Reynard shakes her head, tears gathering in her eyes.

"It's supposed to take a long time, but it didn't. I freaked out. I panicked. I ran downstairs. I got the truck. I wrapped her up in a sheet and I drove for a while on the 101 all the way to downtown. I had no idea where I was going. So, I started driving back. There was an accident and I saw a bunch of cops and I got scared. So, I pulled off the freeway. I drove into LA and to Runyon Canyon, somewhere where she has never been. I dropped her off there."

"You didn't just drop her off," Mrs. Reynard whispers.

“I had to make it look like something else happened,” he says quietly almost under his breath.

"You hung her on that tree?" Mrs. Reynard moans. “Our daughter?"

It hasn't occurred to her, the extent of what Dr. Reynard did yet, but it does to me.

"I had some rope from that shed project you've been on my case about for months. I just wanted to make it look like it wasn't me. I couldn't deal with it anymore. I had to make it look like it was a stranger. I thought that maybe it would be one of those guys that she was talking to. I don't know."

"You staged the crime scene?" Mrs. Reynard asks. "You just hung our daughter out there on that tree and you left her there all night long?"

"I had to protect myself, Maureen. It was an accident. She was already dead."

"No, she wasn't," I interject.

His eyes narrow.

He swallows hard.

"Why don't you tell your wife the truth?"

Dr. Reynard turns his face toward his wife’s.

"I thought she was dead at the house, but she must have just passed out. I took her pulse, but I couldn't feel anything. When I hung her there, she started flailing around."

"Why didn't you let her go?"

"It was too late, Maureen. She knew what I'd done. Don't you get that?" His voice cracks and he buries his head in his hands.

"You killed her. You killed our daughter!" Maureen yells at the top of her lungs.

A shot goes off. Then another.

They're muffled, but still thunderous. I jump back and hide. I pull out my gun, point it, and extend my hand.

"Put your gun down!" I yell.

She moves away from him and I see him, his body crumbled to the floor. Mrs. Reynard is covered in blood.

She had grabbed the gun from her husband and shot him in the chest twice. I walk over to check for his pulse but he's dead.

She melts down onto the floor close to him, but not touching. Her son runs over and grabs onto her. She begins to cry big loud sobs, the kind that leave her gasping for air.

25

As it turned out, Jesse had an alibi for that night, and he wasn't lying. He was also stupid enough to tell Courtney the login information for his account before they ever met. Computer analysis confirmed that she had logged into his account that night from her computer and Dr. Reynard must have seen her do it, which caused them to get into a fight.

Pellegrino went to talk to a girl he'd met at the same Starbucks and they found both of them on camera.

Both times.

First talking to Courtney, the night of her disappearance and then the night of her disappearance to the new girl, who wasn't underage.

We also tracked his phone GPS and confirmed his location.

Dr. Reynard's GPS however, told a completely different story. He hadn't turned it off when he went to drop his daughter's body off in Runyon Canyon Park. He was there.

As far as the cameras around the Reynards' house are concerned, Dr. Reynard must have erased all the info and recorded himself coming back in without her.

I arrested Mrs. Reynard and she's currently being held in jail, awaiting her bail hearing. The prosecutor is keen to take this case to trial but I suspect that she'll plead guilty in exchange for some leniency.

Dennis, their little boy who saw a lot, and heard even more, was taken into child protective services, temporarily, until his grandmother could pick him up and take him home.

As I finish filling out the last of the report, Captain Medvil stops by my desk to congratulate me and to check on how I'm doing.

"That could have ended very badly, Kaitlyn," Captain Medvil says. "You should not have gone there by yourself."

I shrug, trying not to make light of my mistake.

"I just wanted to talk to her and get a little bit more information, maybe another lead to go on," I say, downplaying the whole thing.

"Of course, you had your weapon on you?" he asks rhetorically, even though he already knows the answer.

"I couldn't kill him, not with his son watching," I say, flashing back to the gun pressing against my temple and its unforgettable scent of aluminum.

"I know that it was against procedure. I should have called it in, but I had to take a chance and try to get him to admit it on the recording," I add, shaking my head.

"An easy death is too good for that scum," the captain mutters. "But you could've been killed. You can't take risks like that… What about the wife?"

"I don't think Mrs. Reynard knew anything. She looked shocked."

"You sure?"

I nod confidently. "She had no idea what her husband was capable of."

"But why? Why would he do this?" Captain Medvil asks, thinking out loud.

"He's a controlling piece of work who doesn't like his authority questioned. His daughter did that over and over again. She was defiant. You should have seen how angry he got when he was telling me about her impersonating a doctor at his hospital. Livid."

"Yeah, I heard the recording," the Captain adds. "She certainly didn't deserve this."

I keep thinking of how Courtney must have felt when she realized that her father was strangling her.

Then by some miracle waking up only to see him putting a noose around her neck and strangling her again. This time for good.

"Of course not," I agree.

"You should get some rest now," Captain Medvil says. "You did a good job."

He reaches over to a stack of folders on his desk, a sign that it's time for me to go.

"I may have to take a few days off but I can't exactly get any rest."

"That's right, your sister. What's going on with that?" He raises an eyebrow.

"There's a press conference scheduled for tomorrow morning at nine, KTLA and the local NBC and ABC affiliates are going to be there. My mom is doing the talking but I'll be there for support."

"Keep me updated," Captain Medvil says.

I nod and walk out of his office.

"One more thing," he says right before I disappear down the hallway.

I turn to face him.

"Good luck."

When I grab a cup of coffee, my phone rings. It's Mom. I take a deep breath and decide to let it go to voice mail. I just need a minute; a moment to gather my thoughts, to relax, to enjoy some semblance of peace.

As soon as I refuse to take the call, a text message arrives.

Natalie is gone. She didn't come home last night. Same thing that happened to Violet. Call me.

I read the words over and over again.

I got the sense that Natalie was lying when we talked, but that was it.

When I call Captain Talarico, he confirms the news.

Natalie D'Achille disappeared last night, around the same time as Violet. The last thing anyone knows is that she was out with Neil Goss and got dropped off at her home around nine.

She supposedly has her phone with her, but it's off, so no one knows where she is.

"We're getting the FBI involved. Come up here as soon as you can."

THANK YOU FOR READING! I hope you loved Detective Kaitlyn Carr's investigation. The next book in the Kaitlyn Carr series is **GIRL LOST**.

A **newlywed with a secret pregnancy goes missing after a business trip**. Her husband doesn't seem very concerned.

Why didn't he want to report her missing? Where is she? Why was she keeping her pregnancy a secret? **Detective Kaitlyn Carr has to get to the truth.**

But her sister Violet is still missing, and now her friend has disappeared as well…

One-click GIRL LOST now!

Can't get enough of Kaitlyn Carr? Make sure to grab **GIRL HIDDEN (a novella) for FREE!**

A family is found dead in their home. The only survivor is the teenage daughter who managed to escape the burning house.

Who killed them? And why? **Detective Kaitlyn Carr has to bring their killer to justice.**

A year before her disappearance, Violet, Kaitlyn's sister, comes to stay with her after a bad fight with their mom. She can't stand living at home as much as Kaitlyn once did and wants to move in with her.

What happens when the dysfunction of her own family threatens to blow up her face and let the killer off for good?

GRAB GIRL HIDDEN for FREE now!

If you enjoyed this book, please take a moment to write a short review on your favorite book site and maybe recommend it to a friend or two.

You can also join my Facebook group, Kate Gable's Reader Club, for exclusive giveaways and sneak peeks of future books.

WANT TO BE THE FIRST TO KNOW ABOUT MY UPCOMING SALES, NEW RELEASES AND EXCLUSIVE GIVEAWAYS?

Sign up for my newsletter:
https://www.subscribepage.com/kategableviplist

Join my Facebook Group:
https://www.facebook.com/groups/833851020557518

Bonus Points: Follow me on BookBub and Goodreads!

https://www.goodreads.com/author/show/21534224.Kate_Gable

ABOUT KATE GABLE

Kate Gable loves a good mystery that is full of suspense. She grew up devouring psychological thrillers and crime novels as well as movies, tv shows and true crime.

Her favorite stories are the ones that are centered on families with lots of secrets and lies as well as many twists and turns. Her novels have elements of psychological suspense, thriller, mystery and romance.

Kate Gable lives in Southern California with her husband, son, a dog and a cat. She has spent more than twenty years in this area and finds inspiration from its cities, canyons, deserts, and small mountain towns.

Write her here:

Kate@kategable.com

Check out her books here:

www.kategable.com

Sign up for my newsletter:

https://www.subscribepage.com/kategableviplist

Join my Facebook Group:
https://www.facebook.com/
groups/833851020557518

Bonus Points: Follow me on BookBub and Goodreads!

https://www.bookbub.com/authors/kate-gable

https://www.goodreads.com/author/show/
21534224.Kate_Gable

amazon.com/Kate-Gable/e/B095XFCLL7
facebook.com/kategablebooks
bookbub.com/authors/kate-gable
instagram.com/kategablebooks

ALSO BY KATE GABLE

All books are available at ALL major retailers! If you can't find it, please email me at **kate@kategable.com**

Girl Missing (Book 1)

Girl Lost (Book 2)

Girl Found (Book 3)

Girl Taken (Book 4)

Girl Forgotten (Book 5)

Girl Hidden (FREE Novella)

Made in United States
North Haven, CT
20 February 2023